Other Chaucer Titles
Edited by Michael Murphy:

Canterbury Marriage Tales.
A Reader-Friendly Edition.
Published by Conal & Gavin (2000).
ISBN 0-9679557-1-8

Geoffrey Chaucer: The Canterbury Tales.
The General Prologue and Twelve Major Tales
in Modern Spelling.
Published by University Press of America (1991).
ISBN 0-81918149-8

Audio tapes of the book of twelve tales were recorded
by professional actors in modern English pronunciation
and published by Recorded Books, 270 Skipjack Road,
Prince Frederick, MD 20678. ISBN 1-55690-652-8.

Chaucer's **Troilus and Criseyde** and
The Testament of Cresseid by Henryson.
An electronic edition on the World Wide Web (1999).
http://academic.brooklyn.cuny.edu/webcore/murphy/

The Canterbury Tales.
An electronic edition on the World Wide Web (1999).
http://academic.brooklyn.cuny.edu/webcore/murphy/

To Order Additional Copies
of Canterbury Quintet or
Canterbury Marriage Tales,
contact Little Leaf Press, Inc.
P. O. Box 187, Milaca, MN 56353
Toll Free 877-548-2431
Fax (320) 556-3585
http://www.maxminn.com/littleleaf/
littleleaf@maxminn.com

Canterbury Quintet:
The General Prologue and Four Tales

A Reader-Friendly Edition

The General Prologue
and The Tales of
The Miller
The Wife of Bath
The Pardoner and
The Nun's Priest

by Geoffrey Chaucer

Edited by Michael Murphy

LITTLE LEAF PRESS, INC. & CONAL AND GAVIN

© Copyright 2000 by Michael Murphy

Co-Operatively Published by
Little Leaf Press, Inc.
P. O. Box 187, Milaca, MN 56353
877-548-2431, Fax (320) 556-3585
littleleaf@maxminn.com
http://www.maxminn.com/littleleaf/

and Conal and Gavin Press
641 East 24th Street
Brooklyn, New York 11210

ISBN 1-893385-02-7
LCCN: 00-102741

Publisher's Cataloging-In-Publication Data
Provided by Quality Books, Inc.

Chaucer, Geoffrey, d. 1400:
        Canterbury quintet : the general prologue and
    four tales : a reader-friendly edition : the general
    prologue and the tales of The miller, The wife of
    Bath, The pardoner and The nun's priest   /by
    Geoffrey Chaucer ; edited by Michael Murphy.
    -- 1 st ed.
        p. cm.
        Includes bibliographical references.
        LCCN: 00-102741
        ISBN: 1-893385-02-7

        1. Christian pilgrims and pilgrimages--England--
Canterbury--Poetry.   I. Murphy, Michael, 1932-
II.Title

PR1867.M87 2000   821'.1
                                        QBI00-425

*To my wife and sons
in gratitude and love*

Table of Contents

INTRODUCTORY NOTE
to The Canterbury Quintet

This is not a translation. It is Chaucer's original language with only the spelling modified, as in editions of Shakespeare. "The Language of This Edition" and the "Note on How the Text may be Read" have further comments on a later page.[1]

This is a selection, in modern spelling, of four of the most popular stories from Geoffrey Chaucer's *Canterbury Tales*, as told by four of the pilgrims on that famous fictional journey to Canterbury somewhere in the 1390's to the shrine of St. Thomas Becket, who had been martyred there in the year 1170. We have also included much of the General Prologue, an opening section in which the poet describes the Pilgrims and their agreement to tell the tales.

The people in this varied group tell an equally varied selection of tales, some of them in verse, some in prose. There are tales solemn and comic, religious and bawdy; finished and unfinished; romance, beast fable, mock sermon, parody. One of the most surprising tellers of a powerful moral tale is that ugly and unscrupulous man, the Pardoner. Among the comic pieces are the tales of the Miller and the Nun's Priest, and the Prologue of the Wife of Bath. All four are in our selection.

Here we have some of the best tales from the most famous of Chaucer's writings, one of the most famous works in English literature.

---

[1]For a full development of my argument see my articles "On Not Reading Chaucer – Aloud," *Mediaevalia* 9 (1986 for 1983), 205-224 and "On Editing a New Edition of the Canterbury Tales in Modern Spelling," *Chaucer Review* 26 (1991), 48-64. I have since modified my views enough to restore the "pronounced *e*'s" in many words.

BRIEF LIFE OF CHAUCER

Geoffrey Chaucer was born in London in the early 1340's. His father, a prosperous wine merchant, had enough money to provide his son with an education that grounded him solidly in French and Latin, and enough influence to have the boy taken into an aristocratic household for another kind of education that would later fit him for diplomatic, court and public service. The early part of this training he got in the house of Lionel, one of the sons of King Edward III. At the end of that phase of his education, he went to France on one of the military campaigns of the Hundred Years War, but was captured. He was important enough to be ransomed by the king, but not as important as Sir John of Beverley's horse for which the king paid more ransom money than he did for Geoffrey. Some amused remarks have been made by modern students of Chaucer about the king's sense of priorities, but as Professor Lounsbury said while horses were still a functioning part of American life, there has never been a period in the history of our race when the average man could bring the price of a good horse. That still means that the king thought Geoffrey Chaucer was an average man. How unperceptive, we think.

After his rather inglorious military debut, Geoffrey may have been for a year or two a student at one of the Inns of Court, schools which prepared men for careers in law and administration. He married Philippa Roet (or Pan), a woman who had probably served in the household of Lionel and his wife Elizabeth. Philippa's sister was first the mistress and later the wife of John of Gaunt, another son of Edward III, and one of the most powerful men in the land. Already Geoffrey was well connected. In the 1360's Chaucer served on missions abroad for the king several times. In the early 1370's he visited Italy for the first time on a trade mission, and again in 1378. During these trips he made acquaintance with the work of Dante, Boccaccio and Petrarch, all of whom influenced him profoundly.

In the meantime, in 1374 he had been appointed Controller of the Customs in wool, skins and hides at the Port of London, probably both a demanding and remunerative post, and when he was appointed Controller of the Petty Customs on wines in 1382, he no doubt had more work and more money. These posts he kept until about 1386, when he seems to have lost them through a "change in administration."

They were real jobs, and not sinecures. How he wrote as much as he
did while travelling on diplomatic missions or working full time on
the docks is something of a mystery. He himself lifts the veil just a
tiny bit in a passage spoken by the Eagle to Geoffrey in his poem
The House of Fame:

> Thou hearest neither that nor this.
> For when thy labor done all is,
> And hast made all thy reckonings,
> Instead of rest and newe things
> Thou gost home to thy house anon,
> And all as dumb as any stone
> Thou sittest at another book
> Till fully dazed is thy look.

For a man whose reading and writing were done in large part after
his day's work, he produced a prodigious body of poetry of the very
first rank.

For one year in 1386 he was even a Member of Parliament for Kent.
From 1389-91 he was Clerk of the King's Works, in charge of maintain-
ing some of the major royal buildings under the new king, Richard II. In
the rest of the decade of the 1390's he does not seem to have had any
official position, and there is some evidence that he was in serious debt.
One such piece of evidence is a charming "begging poem" that he wrote
"To His Purse", and directed to King Henry IV who had seized power
from Richard II:

> To you, my purse, and to no other wight   *person*
> Complain I, for you be my lady dear.
> I am so sorry now that you be light...
> Me were as lief be laid upon my bier,   *I'd rather*
> For which unto your mercy thus I cry:
> Be heavy again or else must I die.

And so on for three stanzas ending with a direct plea to the King:

> O conqueror of Brute's Albion...   *(Britain)*
> Have mind upon my supplication

He died in 1400, and was buried in Westminster Abbey, the first
occupant of Poet's Corner.

Chaucer lived during trying and sometimes stirring years, and yet
one hears very little of this in his poetry. He was a small boy when the
Black Death struck for the first time in 1348, one of the most fearful
calamities of the Middle Ages. In several visitations the bubonic plague
wiped out at least one third of the population of England, striking quite
democratically at all ranks of society. It must have left powerful memo-
ries, or at least yielded powerful narratives from his elders, yet there is
hardly a reference to this traumatic event in his work. Partly as the result
of the shortage of labor produced by the Black Death, the peasantry
became rather more demanding. Repressive legislation produced only
rebellion, notably the Peasants Revolt of 1381 which threatened the
whole fabric of society. Again there is but one passing mention of it in
Chaucer's work, though some marxist critics profess to hear its muffled
reverberations throughout.

We do hear rather more about the major religious questions that beset
people at the time. The profound dissatisfaction of many people with the
institutional Church is reflected in Chaucer's satiric portraits of clerics
in his *General Prologue* and in some of his tales. But his satire never
shares the vehemence of a reformer like his contemporary John Wycliffe,
a progenitor of the Reformation, who had to be protected from the
wrath of senior churchmen by the power of John of Gaunt. Nor does it
have the impassioned commitment of a different kind of reformer and
different kind of poet, his other contemporary William Langland, author
of *Piers Plowman.*

From his earliest years and over an extended period of time Chaucer had
rather close contact with some of the most elevated and powerful people
in the land, and yet in more than one place in his work he seems to deal
in a very sympathetic way with the idea that true nobility, "gentilesse,"
is not a matter of "gentle" birth, but of moral quality. And his tales of
"churls" (working people) show him at least as much at home with the
world of the working class as with the aristocratic world portrayed in
the Knight's tale. It is as well to remember that he *did* work for years
in the customs at the port of London where he rubbed shoulders with
everyone from common seamen through small-time pirates to merchant
princes, who were often just bigger pirates.

It is hard now, after six hundred years and the writings of many great poets in English, to realize what a phenomenon Chaucer was. Every poet after him has had a great poet before him writing in English from whom to learn and borrow. Chaucer had no predecessor in English, for the literature of pre-conquest England which we call Old English was a closed book to him, and there seems to have been little English literature of any quality between the Norman Conquest and his time. So it is with reason that he is called the Father of English poetry. His only serious models were the great Latin poets of ancient Rome and the vernacular poets of more modern France and Italy. It was probably from the French and Italians that he got the idea for the English iambic pentameter line which he invented, and which is the line of all his major poetry and of almost all other major poetry in English, rhymed or unrhymed, from his day until very recent times, when metrical verse has largely gone out of fashion. He was a diplomat, a senior civil servant who always worked for a living, and a scholar interested not only in poetry, but in science and philosophy. He translated the *Consolations of Philosophy* by Boethius, a book whose influence on him and on the rest of the literate medieval world it would be difficult to overestimate. And, because astronomy was one of his passions, he wrote for his "little son Lewis" a *Treatise on the Astrolabe,* an instrument for studying the heavens. He knew the standard theories on dreams, and the standard authorities on the theological-philosophical problem of Predestination. He was, in fact, the first of a long line of poets in English who were nearly as learned as they were poetically gifted.

The Language of this Edition

Geoffrey Chaucer who wrote the Tales died rather more than 200 years before the death of Shakespeare.

Since living languages are always changing, it follows that Chaucer's language will be more different from ours than Shakespeare's is. This is most noticeable in the medieval spelling that is preserved in most editions of the Tales. By contrast, the spelling in any current edition of Shakespeare is modern, even if some of the words are obsolete. This sensible editorial convention makes it unnecessary for Shakespeare readers to wrestle with the needless difficulties and uncertainties of the actual spelling of Shakespeare's own day. Shakespeare's verse is difficult enough as it is.

By contrast, the archaic spelling in every edition of Chaucer's verse except ours is a severe obstacle for many people who do not want to fight the difficulties of the fourteenth-century spelling of Chaucer any more than the oddities of the sixteenth-century spelling of Shakespeare. That is why the spelling in our printed edition has been modernized **without changing anything else.**

Somewhere near the front of most editions of Chaucer's work there is nearly always a Guide to Chaucer's Pronunciation, and it is customary in college Chaucer classes to insist that the students *pronounce* the words as Chaucer was supposed to have pronounced them. The accuracy of this re-constructed pronunciation is quite dubious, as it is now 600 years since Chaucer was writing, and the evidence from that period of how English was pronounced ranges from slim to non-existent. There is some reason for scholars to try this reconstructed pronunciation, but not enough reason to impose it on general readers and on students most of whom do not intend to be professional medievalists. For readers and listeners interested in how Chaucer's verse **might** have sounded I have provided a rough "phonetic" version of a short passage below.

Phonetic Version	*Hengwrt Manuscript*
Whan that Avril with his shoorez sote-eh	Whan that Auerylle with his shoures soote
The druughth of March hath persèd toe the rote-eh,	The droghte of March / hath perced to the roote
And baathèd every vein in switch licoor	And bathed euery veyne in swich lycour
Of which vertúe engendrèd is the flure,	Of which vertu engendred is the flour
Whan Zephirus ache with his swayt-eh braith,	Whan zephirus eek with his sweete breeth
Inspeerèd hath in every holt and haith	Inspired hath in euery holt and heeth
The tender croppez, and the yung-eh sun-eh	The tendre croppes / and the yonge sonne
Hath in the Ram his hal-f coorse y-run-eh,	Hath in the Ram / his half cours yronne
And smaaleh foolez maaken melody-eh	And smale foweles / maken melodye
That slaipen al the nicked with awpen ee-eh	That slepen al the nyght with open Iye
So pricketh hem Nat-yóor in hir cooráhjez—	So priketh hem nature / in hir corages
Than longen fol-k to gawn on pilgrimáhjez	Thanne longen folk to goon on pilrymages
And pal-mers for to saiken straunj-eh strondez	And Palmeres for to seeken straunge strondes
To ferneh halwehs couth in sundry londez	To fernè halwes / kouthe in sondry londes
And spesyaly from every sheerez end-eh	And specially / from euery shyres ende
Of Engelond to Caunterbry they wend-eh	Of Engelond / to Caunterbury they wende
The hawly blissful martyr for to saik-eh	The holy blisful martir / for to seke
That hem hath holpen whan that they were saik-eh.	That hem hath holpen whan at they weere seeke.

This passage and others are reproduced in the International Phonetic Alphabet in Helge Kokeritz's pamphlet *A Guide To Chaucer's Pronunciation* (Holt, Rinehart: N.Y., 1962). Even in Kokeritz, which is the standard version, the uncertainties of the phonetics are clear from the fact that he gives fifteen alternative pronunciations in sixteen lines. The Chaucer Studio has produced tape recordings of many of the tales by academics spoken in this reconstructed dialect.(Department of English, Brigham Young University, Provo, Utah 84602).

The conviction behind this present edition is that Chaucer can be read in standard modern spelling, and heard in any standard spoken English. And by Chaucer we mean the language of Chaucer himself, NOT a translation. The language of this edition is **Chaucer's** language line for line, word for word — Chaucer's vocabulary, Chaucer's word order, Chaucer's sentence structure. The only things that we have modernized, in accordance with the practice for all other authors, are spelling and punctuation. But this makes all the difference.

Some obsolete and archaic words and forms remain, but this is true of the work of any author from a former era, and even with an author as old as Chaucer these expressions are never so numerous as to hold up seriously the meaning of the narrative. Moreover, **all unusual words are glossed** in the right margin. But it is probably unwise and certainly unnecessary to stop your reading to look up **every** unfamiliar word or for other small difficulties. The narrative itself will often explain these.

There are tape recordings by professional actors of the tales as printed in this edition (for details of Recorded Books see p. 2 above). Listeners without any acquaintance with the theories of Middle English sounds can enjoy the tales spoken in modern English. A combination of the tape and the edition is an excellent way to get a good grasp of Chaucer's work with a minimum of wrestling with the oddities of spoken or written Middle English, as Chaucer's English is called. The tapes are especially useful for those who have to use an old-spelling edition so that they can listen to the modern pronunciation while reading the old spelling. Much of the pain of fighting the archaic spelling and sounds is thus eliminated, so readers and hearers learn quickly to **enjoy** Chaucer not merely endure him. The poetry remains great after the elimination, of the difficulty of old spelling and old pronunciation, a difficulty that did not exist, remember, for Chaucer's contemporaries.

A Note on How the Text may be Read

The written text is a compromise between the forms of Middle and Modern English.

The reader is invited, though not pressed, to pronounce (silently or aloud) all instances of dotted e as in "Inspirèd", "easèd", "youngè", "sunnè".

This superscript dot indicates a letter that was probably pronounced in Chaucer's medieval poetic dialect, possibly with a light schwa sound, a kind of brief "-uh". Hence, this newspell text has kept some medieval spellings that differ somewhat from ours: "sweetè" for "sweet", "halfè" for "half", "couldè" for "could", "lippès" for "lips", and so on. This preserves the extra syllable to indicate the more regular meter that many scholars insist was Chaucer's, and that many readers will prefer. The reader is the final judge.

It is quite possible to read "With locks curled as they were laid in press" rather than "With lockės curled as they were laid in press." Some would prefer "She let no morsel from her lips fall" over "She let no morsel from her lippės fall". Similarly a sentence of strong monosyllables like "With scaled brows black and piled beard" should be at least as good as "With scalėd browės black and pilėd beard." There is nothing to prevent any reader with similar tastes from doing the same, that is, ignoring the dotted ė whenever you feel that is appropriate. The text offers a choice. Blameth not me if that you choose amiss.

Similarly one may wish to pronounce the ï of "natïons", to make three syllables for the word instead of two, "condïtïon" with four syllables instead of three, etc.

The medieval endings of some words, especially verbs, in -n or -en have been retained for reasons of smoother rhythm: **"sleepen, seeken, weren, woulden, liven, withouten."** Such words mean the same with or without the -n or -en, and Chaucer used or omitted the endings as suited his poetic purpose. Also words beginning y- mean the same with or without the y- as in **y-tied, y-taught**. The y- is simply a sign of the past participle.

An acute accent indicates that a word was probably stressed in a different (French) way from its modern counterpart as in these rhyming pairs: **uságe, viságe; daggér, mannér; serviceáble, table; dance, penánce; alas, soláce**. These originally French words almost certainly retained more of their French pronunciation in Chaucer's day than they do now. But the reader should feel free to disregard these and all other superscript markings.

Archaic words or phrases have been over-glossed rather than under-glossed. That is, many words are glossed again and again in the margins because I do not know that every reader will choose to proceed from beginning to end, but may start somewhere in the middle. After a while, when much of the vocabulary will have been absorbed, the reader should ignore the marginal glosses except when absolutely necessary.

The line numbers are those of the sections as published in the Riverside, the standard scholarly edition.

THE GENERAL PROLOGUE

Introduction

The Canterbury Tales begins with a General Prologue in which the poet tells us how he happened to meet these "nine and twenty" pilgrims on the way to Canterbury, how they agreed to tell the tales at the suggestion of the landlord of The Tabard (the inn where they stopped in Southwark in south London), and how they all appeared to the poet: their habits, their speech, their clothes, their attitudes, and so forth.

It has often been remarked, and it is worth remarking again, that this portrait gallery provides a wonderful cross section of fourteenth-century English society. Not a complete and comprehensive survey, for Chaucer is a poet not a sociologist, but it is a sampling remarkable for its diversity: there are men and women, clerics and laymen; young, middle aged and old; people who differ widely in their spiritual lives, their economic status, their tastes in clothes, books, and food; those who need to travel constantly and those for whom this will be the one major journey of their life. There are rogues and innocents, introverts and show-offs, saints (few) and sinners (many).

Most of these portraits are here, sometimes lightly abbreviated, but I have taken the descriptions of the Miller, the Wife and the Pardoner from their place among the others in the General Prologue, and have put them just before their individual Tales. Oddly, Chaucer did not provide any pen portrait of that very charming storyteller the Nun's Priest.

GENERAL PROLOGUE

The opening is a long, elaborate sentence about the effects of Spring on the vegetable and animal world, and on people. The style of the rest of the Prologue and Tales is much simpler than this opening. A close paraphrase of the opening sentence is offered at the bottom of this page.[1]

	When that April with his showers soot	*its sweet showers*
	The drought of March hath piercèd to the root	
	And bathèd every vein in such liqúor	*rootlet / liquid*
	Of which virtúe engendered is the flower	
5	When Zephyrus eke with his sweetè breath	*West Wind also*
	Inspirèd hath in every holt and heath	*grove & field*
	The tender croppès, and the youngè sun	*young shoots / Spring sun*
	Hath in the Ram his halfé course y-run,	*in Aries / Has ... run*
	And smallè fowlès maken melody	*little birds*
	That sleepen all the night with open eye	*sleep*
	So pricketh them Natúre in their couráges),	*N. spurs them / spirits*
	Then longen folk to go on pilgrimages,	*people long*
	And palmers for to seeken strangè strands	*pilgrims / shores*
	To fernè hallows couth in sundry lands,	*distant shrines known*
15	And specially from every shirè's end	*county's*
	Of Engèland to Canterbury they wend	*they go*
	The holy blissful martyr for to seek,	*[St. Thomas Becket]*
	That them hath holpen when that they were sick.	*helped*

---

[1] When April with its sweet showers has pierced the drought of March to the root, and bathed every rootlet in the liquid by which the flower is engendered; when the west wind also, with its sweet breath, has brought forth young shoots in every grove and field; when the early sun of spring has run half his course in the sign of Aries, and when small birds make melody, birds that sleep all night with eyes open, (as Nature inspires them to) —THEN people have a strong desire to go on pilgrimages, and pilgrims long to go to foreign shores to distant shrines known in various countries. And especially they go from every county in England to seek out the shrine of the holy blessed martyr who has helped them when they were sick.

At the Tabard Inn, just south of London, the poet-pilgrim
falls in with a group of twenty nine other pilgrims
who have met each other along the way.

Befell that in that season on a day	*It happened*
20 In Southwark at The Tabard as I lay	*Tabard = inn name / lodged*
Ready to wenden on my pilgrimage	*to go*
To Canterbury with full devout couráge,	*spirit, heart*
At night was come into that hostelry	*inn*
Well nine and twenty in a company	*fully 29*
Of sundry folk by áventure y-fall	*by chance joined...*
In fellowship, and pilgrims were they all	*...in company*
That toward Canterbury woulden ride.	*wished to*
The chambers and the stables weren wide	*were roomy*
And well we weren easéd at the best.	*were entertained*
30 And shortly, when the sunné was to rest,	*sun had set*
So had I spoken with them every one	
That I was of their fellowship anon,	
And madé forward early for to rise	*agreement*
To take our way there as I you devise.	*I shall tell you*
But natheless, while I have time and space,	*nevertheless*
Ere that I further in this talé pace,	*Before I go*
Methinketh it accordant to reason	*It seems to me reasonable*
To tell you all the condition	*circumstances*
Of each of them so as it seeméd me,	*to me*
40 And which they weren, and of what degree	*social rank*
And eke in what array that they were in;	*And also / dress*
And at a knight then will I first begin.	

The Knight *is the person of highest social standing on the pilgrimage*
though you would never know it from his modest manner or his clothes.
He keeps his ferocity for crusaders' battlefields where he has distinguished
himself over many years and over a wide geographical area. As the text
says, he is not "gay", that is, he is not showily dressed, but is still wearing
the military padded coat stained by the armor he has only recently
taken off.

A KNIGHT there was and that a worthy man		
That from the timė that he first began		
To riden out, he lovėd chivalry,		
Truth and honóur, freedom and courtesy.[1]		
Full worthy was he in his lordė's war,		
And thereto had he ridden—no man farre		*farther*
As well in Christendom as Heatheness		*heathendom*
50 And ever honoured for his worthiness.		
At Alexandria he was when it was won.		*captured*
Full often time he had the board begun		*headed the table*
Aboven allė natïons in Prussia.[2]		
In Lithow had he reisėd and in Russia		*Lithuania / fought*
No Christian man so oft of his degree.		*rank*
And ever more he had a sovereign prize,[3]		*always*
And though that he was worthy he was wise,		*valiant / sensible*
And of his port as meek as is a maid.		*deportment*
70 Ne never yet no villainy he said		*rudeness*
In all his life unto no manner wight.[4]		*no kind of person*
He was a very perfect gentle knight.		

---

[1] 45-7: "He loved everything that pertained to knighthood: truth (to one's word), honor, magnanimity (*freedom*), courtesy." *His lord* may be his lord God or his lord the king.

[2] 52-3: He had often occupied the seat of honor at the table of the Teutonic Knights in Prussia. The names of some of his more obscure campaigns are omitted here. This portrait is generally thought to show a man of unsullied ideals; Terry Jones insists that he was a mere mercenary.

[3] 67: "*And ever more ...*" may mean he always kept the highest reputation or that he always came away with a splendid reward or booty.

[4] 70-71: Notice quadruple negative: "*ne, never, no, no*" used for emphasis, perhaps deliberately excessive emphasis. It is not bad grammar.

But for to tellen you of his array
His horse was good; but *he* was not gay[1]   *well dressed*
For he was late y-come from his voyage,   *just come*
And wentė for to do his pilgrimage.[2]

*The Knight's 20-year-old son is a striking contrast to his father.
True, he has seen some military action, but it was to impress his lady
not his Lord God. Unlike his parent, he is fashionably dressed; he is
very much in love, he has cultivated all the social graces, and is
also aware of his duty to serve as his father's squire.*

With him there was his son, a young SQUIRE,
80   A lover and a lusty bachelor[3]
With lockės curled as they were laid in press.   *as if in curlers*
Of twenty years he was of age, I guess.
And he had been sometime in chivachy   *campaign*
In Flanders, in Artois and Picardy,
And borne him well as in so little space[4]   *conducted / time*
In hope to standen in his lady's grace.   *good graces*
Embroidered was he as it were a mead   *meadow*
90   All full of freshė flowers white and red.
Singing he was or fluting all the day.   *whistling?*
He was as fresh as is the month of May.
Short was his gown with sleevės long and wide.
Well could he sit on horse and fairė ride.
He couldė songės make and well endite,   *write words & music*
Joust and eke dance, and well portray and write.   *also / draw*

---

[1] 74: "he" = the Knight. *horse was* (MS Lansdowne); most MSS read *hors weere(n)* = "horses were." The knight is more interested in the quality of his horse than of his clothes.

[2] 75-78: The poor state of the knight's clothes is generally interpreted to indicate his pious anxiety to fulfill a religious duty even before he has had a chance to change. Jones thinks it simply confirms that the knight was a mercenary who had pawned his armor. *voyage:* MSS have *viage. Blessed viage* was the term often used for the holy war of the crusades.

[3] 79-80: A squire learned his future duties as a knight by attending on one. *Bachelor* is another word meaning a young man in training to be a knight.

[4] 87: "And distinguished himself, considering the short time he had been at it."

So hot he lovèd that by nightertale   *night*
He slept no more than does a nightingale.
Courteous he was, lowly and serviceable,
100 And carved before his father at the table.[1]

*Knight and Squire are accompanied by their **Yeoman** whose portrait is here omitted. He is noticeably overarmed for a pilgrimage, which indicates probably suspicion of the big city by a man more at home in the forest.*

***The Prioress** is the head of a fashionable convent. She is a charming lady, none the less charming for her slight worldliness: she has a romantic name, Eglantine, wild rose; she has delicate table manners and is exquisitely sensitive to animal rights; she speaks French — after a fashion; she has a pretty face and knows it; her nun's habit is elegantly tailored, and she displays discreetly a little tasteful jewelry: a gold brooch on her rosary embossed with the nicely ambiguous Latin motto: Amor Vincit Omnia, Love conquers all.*

There was also a nun, a PRIORESS,   *head of a convent*
And she was clepèd Madame Eglantine.   *called*
Full well she sang the servicè divine
Entunèd in her nose full seemèly.[2]
And French she spoke full fair and fetisly   *nicely*
After the school of Stratford at the Bow,
For French of Paris was to her unknown.[3]
At meatè well y-taught was she withall: *meals / indeed*
She let no morsel from her lippès fall,
Nor wet her fingers in her saucè deep.
130 Well could she carry a morsel and well keep   *handle*
That no drop fell upon her breast.   *So that*
In courtesy was set full much her lest: *very much her interest*
Her over lippè wipèd she so clean   *upper lip*

---

[1] 100: The table would usually be occupied at only one side, so when the Squire carved for his father, the Knight, he stood before him across the table.

[2] 123: A joke presumably, not adequately explained.

[3] 126: This is a snigger at the provincial quality of the lady's French, acquired not in Paris but in a London suburb, Stratford at the Bow. Everything about the prioress is meant to suggest affected elegance of a kind not especially appropriate in a nun: her facial features, her manners, her jewelry, her French, her clothes, her name. *Eglantine* = "wild rose" or "sweet briar." *Madame* = "my lady."

That in her cup there was no farthing seen   *small stain*
135 Of greasė, when she drunkėn had her draught.
Full seemėly after her meat she raught,[1]   *food / reached*
And painėd her to counterfeitė cheer   *imitate manners*
Of court,[2] and be estately of mannėr,   *dignified*
And to be holden digne of reverence.   *thought worthy*

She is very sensitive

But for to speaken of her conscïence: *sensitivity*
She was so charitable and so pitous   *compassionate*
She wouldė weep if that she saw a mouse
Caught in a trap, if it were dead or bled.
Of smallė houndės had she that she fed   *dogs*
With roasted flesh or milk and wastel bread,   *fine bread*
But sore wept she if one of them were dead
Or if men smote it with a yardė, smart;   *w. a stick smartly*
150 And all was conscïence and tender heart.

Her personal appearance

Full seemėly her wimple pinchėd was,   *headdress pleated*
Her nose tretis, her eyen grey as glass,   *handsome / eyes*
Her mouth full small and thereto soft and red,   *and also*
But sikerly she had a fair forehead.   *certainly*
It was almost a spannė broad, I trow,   *handsbreadth / I guess*
For hardily she was not undergrow.   *certainly / short? thin?*
Full fetis was her cloak as I was 'ware.   *elegant / aware*
Of small coral about her arm she bare   *bore, carried*
A pair of beads gauded all with green,   *A rosary decorated*
160 And thereon hung a brooch of gold full sheen   *shining*
On which was written first a crownėd A
And after: Amor Vincit Omnia.[3]

     Love Conquers All

---

[1] 136 In a very mannerly way she reached for her food (*meat*).

[2] 138-39: She took pains to imitate the manners of the (king's) court.

[3] 161-2: Her gold brooch had a capital "A" with a crown above it, and a Latin motto meaning "Love conquers all," a phrase appropriate to both sacred and secular love. It occurs in a French poem that Chaucer knew well, *The Romance of the Rose* (21327-32), where Courteoisie quotes it from Virgil's "Eclogue" X, 69, to justify the plucking of the Rose by the Lover, a decidedly secular, indeed sexual, act of "Amor".

*Another member of the church is the **Monk** who, like the Prioress,
is supposed to stay in his monastery but who, like her, finds an excuse
to get away from it, something he does a lot. He has long since lost any
of the monastic ideals he may have set out with, and he now prefers
travel, good clothes, good food, good hunting with well-equipped horses,
in place of the poverty, study and manual labor prescribed by his monastic
rule. He may not be a bad man, but he is not a good monk.*

	A MONK there was, a fair for the mastery,	*a fine fellow*
	An outrider that lovèd venery.[1]	*horseman / hunting*
	A manly man to be an abbot able,	
	Full many a dainty horse had he in stable,	
	And when he rode, men might his bridle hear	
170	Jingle in a whistling wind as clear	
	And eke as loud as does the chapel bell	*And also*
	There as this lord is keeper of the cell.[2]	*Where / annex*
	The rule of Saintè Maur or of Saint Bennett	*[monastic] rule*
	Because that it was old and somedeal strait	*somewhat strict*
	This ilkè monk let oldè thingès pass	*This same / go*
	And held after the newè world the space.	*modern ways now*

The poet pretends to agree with his lax views

	And I said his opinïon was good;	*I = narrator*
	What! should he study and make himselfen wood	*himself mad*
	Upon a book in cloister always to pore?	
	Or swinken with his handès and laboúr	*or work*
	As Austin bids? How shall the world be served?	*St Augustine*
	Let Austin have his swink to him reserved.[3]	

The Monk's taste in sport and clothes

	Therefore he was a prickasour aright.	*a hunter for sure*
190	Greyhounds he had as swift as fowl in flight.	
	Of pricking and of hunting for the hare	*tracking*

---

[1] 166: *venery* = both "hunting" and the work of Venus, goddess of love. This description of the Monk is larded with sexual innuendo.

[2] 172: The monk is in charge of an annex (*cell*) of the monastery.

[3] 188: "Let Augustine keep his work." An unbecoming way for a monk to speak of the great saint whose rule, like that of St. Maurus and St. Benedict (*Maur* and *Bennett*, 173) prescribed study and physical labor for monks.

Was all his lust, for no cost would he spare. *passion*
I saw his sleevės purfled at the hand *edged at the wrist*
With gris, and that the finest of the land, *fur*
And for to fasten his hood under his chin
He had of gold wrought a full curious pin — *very elaborate*
A love-knot on the greater end there was.

His appearance

His head was bald, that shone as any glass
And eke his face, as he had been anoint. *also / as if oiled*
He was a lord full fat and in good point. *in good health*
His boots supple, his horse in great estate. *in great shape*
Now certainly he was a fair prelate. *cleric*
205 He was not pale as is a forpined ghost. *tortured*
A fat swan loved he best of any roast.
His palfrey was as brown as any berry. *horse*

The Friar, *another cleric, is even less a man of God than the Monk. A member of a mendicant order of men who lived on what they could get by begging, he has become a professional fund-raiser, the best in his friary because of some special skills: personal charm, a good singing voice, an attractive little lisp, a talent for mending quarrels and having the right little gift for the ladies, and a forgiving way in the confessional especially when he expects a generous donation. He can find good economic reasons to cultivate the company of the rich rather than the poor.*

A FRIAR there was, a wanton and a merry, *lively*
A limiter, a full solémpnė man.[1]
In all the orders four is none that can *knows*
So much of dalliance and fair language. *smooth manners*
He had made full many a marrïage
Of youngė women at his ownė cost.[2]
Unto his order he was a noble post. *pillar*

---

[1] 208-9: "There was a very cheerful and lively Friar who was a licensed mendicant, a very striking man." A Friar (Fr. *frère*) was a member of one of four religious orders of men. Our friar, a *limiter*, has a begging district within which he is licensed to beg. *Solempne* cannot mean "solemn" except as heavy irony.

[2] 212-13: He had performed the marriage ceremonies without a fee or he had provided dowries for many young women. Why a mendicant would provide girls with dowries is a question that has invited speculation about the friar's possible sexual activity.

215   Full well beloved and familiar was he
    With franklins over all in his country,   *landowners*
    And eke with worthy women of the town.   *also*

His manner in the confessional

    Full sweetėly heard he confessïon
    And pleasant was his absolutïon.
    He was an easy man to give penánce
    There as he wist to have a good pittánce,   *expected a g. offering*
    Therefore, instead of weeping and prayers
    Men may give silver to the poorė freres.   *friars*

The company he cultivated

    His tipet was ay farsėd full of knives   *hood was always packed*
    And pinnės for to given fairė wives.   *pins*
    And certainly he had a merry note—
    Well could he sing and playen on a rote.   *stringed instrument*
240   He knew the taverns well in every town
    And every hosteler and tappester   *innkeeper & barmaid*
    Bet than a lazar or a beggester,[1]   *Better / leper / beggar*
    For unto such a worthy man as he
    Accorded not as by his faculty   *Didn't suit his rank*
    To have with sickė lazars ácquaintance.   *lepers*
    It is not honest, it may not advance   *proper / profit*
    For to dealen with no such poraille,   *poor people*
    But all with rich and sellers of vitaille.   *food*

His begging manner was so smooth, he could, if necessary, extract money from the poorest

    He was the bestė beggar in his house:
    For though a widow haddė not a shoe,
    So pleasant was his "In Principio"   *his blessing*
255   Yet he would have a farthing ere he went.   *1/4 of a penny*
    His purchase was well better than his rent.[2]

---

[1] 241-2: *Tapster, beggester:* the *-ster* ending signified, strictly, a female. It survives (barely) in *spinster.* Cultivating innkeepers and barmaids paid better than loving lepers or beggars.

[2] 256: His income (*purchase*) from the begging was much larger than his outlay (*rent*) for the monopoly in the district.

And he had other talents and attractions

And rage he could as it were right a whelp.	*frolic like a puppy*
In lovèdays there could he muchel help,	*mediation days*
For there he was not like a cloisterer[1]	
With a threadbare cope as is a poorè scholar,	*cloak*
But he was like a master or a pope.[2]	
Of double worsted was his semi-cope,	*short cloak*
And rounded as a bell out of the press.	*the mold*
Somewhat he lispèd for his wantonness	*affectation*

265 To make his English sweet upon his tongue,

And in his harping when that he had sung,	*harp-playing*
His eyen twinkled in his head aright	*eyes*
As do the starrès in the frosty night.	*stars*
This worthy limiter was cleped Hubert.	*was called*

The Merchant, *whose portrait we omit, is apparently a prosperous exporter who likes to TALK of his prosperity; he is concerned about pirates and profits, skillful in managing exchange rates, but tightlipped about business details.*

The Clerk *is the first admirable church member we meet on the pilgrimage. "Clerk" meant a number of related things: a cleric, a student, a scholar. This clerk is all three, devoted to the love of learning and of God, the quintessential scholar, totally unworldly, who would rather buy a book than a coat or a good meal.*

285 A CLERK there was of Oxenford also	*Oxford*
That unto logic haddè long y-go.[3]	*gone*

---

[1] 259: *cloisterer*: probably a "real" friar who stayed largely within his cloister, satisfied with poor clothes according to his vow of poverty. *Lovedays* were days for out-of-court settlements. The Friar was evidently a good mediator on such days, partly because of his impressively good clothes, apparently.

[2] 261: *master*: possibly Master of Arts, a rather more eminent degree than it is now, though hardly making its holder as exalted as the pope.

[3] 285-6: He had long since set out to study logic, part of the *trivium* or lower section of the university syllabus (the other two parts of the trivium were rhetoric and grammar); hence his early college years had long since passed. The higher section was the *quadrivium*: arithmetic, geometry, music, astronomy. *y-go* = "gone", the past participle of "go".

As leanė was his horse as is a rake,	
And he was not right fat, I undertake,	*he = the Clerk*
But lookėd hollow, and thereto soberly.	*gaunt & also serious*
290 Full threadbare was his overest courtepy,	*outer cloak*
For he had gotten him yet no benefice	*parish*
Nor was so worldly for to have office,	*secular job*
For him was lever have at his bed's head	*For he would rather*
Twenty bookės clad in black or red	*bound*
Of Aristotle and his philosophy	
Than robės rich or fiddle or gay psalt'ry.	*stringed instrument*
But albeit that he was a philosopher,	*although*
Yet haddė he but little gold in coffer,[1]	*chest*
But all that he might of his friendės hent	*get*
300 On bookės and on learning he it spent,	
And busily gan for the soulės pray	*regulary prayed for*
Of them that gave him wherewith to scholay.	*study*
Of study took he most care and most heed.	
Not one word spoke he morė than was need,	
And that was spoke in form and reverence,	
And short and quick and full of high senténce.	*lofty thought*
Sounding in moral virtue was his speech,	
And gladly would he learn and gladly teach.	

Several more portraits are here omitted:

The Sergeant of the Law *is a successful but unostentatious, high-ranking lawyer who sometimes functions as a judge. We are told with just a touch of irony, that he is, like many of the pilgrims, the very best at what he does, a busy man, but "yet he* **seemėd** *busier than he was."*

The Lawyer is accompanied by his friend, the **Franklin,** *a prosperous country gentleman, prominent in his county. He is a generous extroverted man ("sanguine" the text says) who likes good food and drink and sharing them with others, somewhat like St Julian, the patron saint of hospitality.*

---

[1] 298: A joke. Although he was a student of philosophy, he had not discovered the "philosopher's stone," which was supposed to turn base metals into gold. The two senses of "philosopher" played on here are: a) student of the work of Aristotle b) student of science ("natural philosophy"), a meaning which shaded off into "alchemist, magician." In Chaucer's dialect *philosópher* was probably stressed thus on the third syllable, French fashion.

Somewhat lower in the social scale is a group of **Skilled Tradesmen**
most of them connected with the fabric trades and belonging to a guild,
a "fraternity". Their prosperity shows in their clothes, and their accou-
trements and the fact that they have brought their own cook perhaps to
replace the skills of the ambitious wives they have left at home.

The **Shipman** *is a ship's captain, the most skilled from here to Spain, more*
at home on the deck of ship than on the back of a horse. He is not above a
little larceny or piracy and in a sea fight he does not take prisoners.

The medical **Doctor** *is, of course, the best in his profession, and though*
his practice, typical of the period, sounds to us more like astrology and
magic than medicine, he makes a very good living at it.

The **Wife of Bath***'s portrait will be found just before her tale below.*

The second good cleric we meet is more than good; he is near perfection.
The priest of a small, obscure and poor parish in the country the **Parson**
ministers to his flock without any worldly ambition. He has not forgotten
the lowly class from which he came. Unlike most of the other pilgrims, he
is not physically described, perhaps because he is such an ideal figure.

	A good man was there of Religïon	
	And was a poorë PARSON of a town,	*parish priest*
	But rich he was of holy thought and work.	
480	He was also a learnëd man, a clerk,	*a scholar*
	That Christë's gospel truly wouldë preach.	
	His parishens devoutly would he teach.	*parishioners*
	Benign he was and wonder diligent	*wonderfully*
	And in adversity full patïent.	
	Wide was his parish and houses far asunder	
	But he ne leftë not, for rain nor thunder	*did not fail*
	In sickness nor in mischief, to visit	
	The furthest in his parish, much and little,	*rich and poor*
	Upon his feet, and in his hand a stave.	*stick*
	This noble example unto his sheep he gave	
	That first he wrought and afterwards he taught:	*practiced*
	Out of the gospel he those wordës caught	
	And this figúre he added eke thereto:	*this saying*
500	"That if gold rustë, what shall iron do?"[1]	

---

[1] 500 "If *gold* rusts, what will happen to iron?" A proverb in the form of a
rhetorical question.

For if a priest be foul (in whom we trust)
No wonder is a lewèd man to rust   *layman*
And shame it is, if that a priest take keep,   *thinks about it*
A shiten shepherd and a cleanè sheep.   *dirty*
Well ought a priest example for to give
By his cleanness, how that his sheep should live.
To drawen folk to heaven with fairness
By good example, this was his business.
But it were any person obstinate,   *But if*
What so he were of high or low estate,   *Whether*
Him would he snibben sharply for the nonès.   *rebuke / occasion*
A better priest I trow there nowhere none is.   *I guess*
And Christ's lore, and his apostles' twelve   *teaching*
He taught, but first he followed it himself.[1]

The Parson's brother, the **Plowman,** *probably the lowest in
social rank on the pilgrimage, is one of the highest in spirituality,
the perfect lay Christian, the secular counterpart of his cleric brother.*

      With him there was a PLOUGHMAN was his brother   *who was*
530   That had y-laid of dung full many a fodder.   *spread / a load*
      A true swinker and a good was he,   *worker*
      Living in peace and perfect charity.
      God loved he best with all his wholè heart
      At allè timès, though him gamed or smart,   *pleased or hurt*
      And then his neighèbour right as himself.

*We now come to a group of rogues and churls with whom the poet
amusingly lumps himself: the Reeve, the Miller, the Summoner, the
Pardoner, the Manciple, and "myself", he says. You may well ask what
some of these people are doing on a* **pilgrimage.**

The **Miller***'s portrait is found below just before his tale.*

---

[1] 527-8: "He taught Christ's doctrine (*lore*) and that of His twelve apostles, but first he practised it himself."

*The **Manciple** is in charge of buying provisions for a group of Lawyers in London, but is shrewder in his management than all of them put together.*

*The **Reeve** manages an estate for a young lord of whom he takes advantage, though he makes sure that no one takes advantage of **him**. He is an old, choleric man, that is, he has a short temper that goes with his skinny frame and his suspicious mind. He always rides at the end of the procession.*

*The **Summoner** is a man who delivers summonses to people to appear at the ecclesiastical court when accused of public immorality. The job offered opportunities for serious abuse such as bribery, extortion, and especially blackmail of those who went with prostitutes many of whom the summoner used himself, and all of them in his pay. His disgusting physical appearance is meant to suggest his wretched spiritual condition.*

	A SUMMONER was there with us in that place	
	That had a fire-red cherubinnė's face,[1]	*cherub's*
625	For saucéfleme he was with eyen narrow.	*leprous / eyes*
	And hot he was and lecherous as a sparrow.[2]	
	With scalėd browės black, and pilėd beard,	*scaly / scraggly*
	Of his viságė children were afeared.	
	He was a gentle harlot, and a kind.	*rascal*
	A better fellow shouldė men not find:	
	He wouldė suffer for a quart of wine	*would allow*
	A good fellow to have his concubine	*keep his mistress*
	A twelvemonth, and excuse him at the full.	*let him off completely*
	In daunger had he, at his ownė guise	*In his power / disposal*
635	The youngė girlės of the diocese[3]	
	And knew their counsel and was all their redde.	*secrets / adviser*
	A garland had he set upon his head	
	As great as it were for an alėstake.	*tavern sign*
	A buckler had he made him of a cake.[4]	*shield*

---

[1] 624: Medieval artists painted the faces of cherubs red. The summoner is of course less cherubic than satanic.

[2] 626: Sparrows were Venus's birds, considered lecherous presumably because they were so many.

[3] 635: *girls* probably meant "prostitutes," as it still can.

[4] 639: A tavern sign (*alestake*) was often a large wreath or broom on a pole. Acting the buffoon, the Summoner has also turned a thin cake into a shield.

*With the disgusting Summoner is his friend, his singing partner
and possibly his lover, the even more corrupt **Pardoner,** whose
portrait will be found below just before his prologue and tale.*

The portraits of the pilgrims end here.

715	Now have I told you soothly in a clause	*truly / briefly*
	Th'estate, th'array, the number, and eke the cause	*rank / condition*
	Why that assembled was this company	
	In Southwark at this gentle hostelry	*inn*
	And after will I tell of our viage	*journey*
	And all the remnant of our pilgrimage.	

*The poet offers a comic apologia for the matter and language
of some of the pilgrims. He pretends that he has to be faithful to
the exact words that the pilgrims used. Of course there were no
pilgrims; they are all Chaucer's creation, and so are their words.*

725	But first I pray you of your courtesy	
	That you n'arrette it not my villainy[1]	*not blame / bad manners*
	Though that I plainly speak in this mattér	
	To tellė you their wordės and their cheer,	*behavior*
	Not though I speak their wordės properly,	*exactly*
	For this you knowen all so well as I:	*as well*
	Whoso shall tell a tale after a man[2]	
	He must rehearse as nigh as ever he can	*repeat as nearly*
	Ever each a word, if it be in his charge,	*Every / if he is able*
	All speak he ne'er so rudėly and large,	*Even if / coarsely & freely*
735	Or elsė must he tell his tale untrue	
	Or feignė things or finden wordės new.	*invent things*
	He may not spare, although he were his brother.	*hold back*
	He may as well say one word as another.	
	Christ spoke himself full broad in Holy Writ	*very bluntly / Scripture*
	And well you wot no villainy is it.	*you know*

---

[1] 725-726: "But I beg you, please, not to blame it on my bad manners." *Villainy*
means conduct associated with villeins, the lowest social class.

[2] 731 ff: "Whoever wants to tell a story heard from another man must repeat as
nearly as he can every word, if he is able, even if he speaks ever so coarsely and freely.
If not, he does not tell the tale properly and must invent things or find different words."

After serving dinner, Harry Bailly, the Host or owner of the Tabard Inn
originates the idea for the Tales: to pass the time pleasantly, every one will
tell a couple of tales on the way out and a couple on the way back.

755	Great cheerė made our HOST us every one,[1]	*welcome / for us*
	And to the supper set he us anon.	*quickly*
	He servėd us with victuals at the best.	*the best food*
	Strong was the wine and well to drink us lest.	*it pleased us*
	A seemly man our Hostė was withall	*fit*
	For to be a marshall in a hall.	*master of ceremonies*
	Eke thereto he was right a merry man,	*And besides*
	And after supper playen he began	*to joke*
	And saidė thus: "Now, lordings, truly,	*ladies and g'men*
	I saw not this year so merry a company	
765	At oncė in this harbor as is now.	*this inn*
	Fain would I do you mirthė, wist I how,	*Gladly / if I knew*
	And of a mirth I am right now bethought	*amusement*
	To do you ease, and it shall costė naught.	

	Lordings," quod he, "now hearken for the best,	*Ladies & g'men*
	But take it not, I pray you, in disdain.	
	This is the point — to speaken short and plain:	
	That each of you to shorten with our way	
	In this viage, shall tellen talės tway	*journey / two*
	To Canterbury-ward, I mean it so,	*on the way to C.*
	And homeward he shall tellen other two	
795	Of áventures that whilom have befall.	*events / in past*

The teller of the best tale will get a dinner paid for by all the others
at Harry's inn, The Tabard, on the way back from Canterbury.
He offers to go with them as a guide.

	And which of you that bears him best of all,	*whoever does best*
	That is to say, that telleth in this case	
	Talės of best senténce and most soláce,	*instruction / amusement*
	Shall have a supper at our aller cost	*at expense of all of us*
800	Here in this place, sitting by this post	*this pillar*
	When that we come again from Canterbury.	

---

[1] 755: "The Host had a warm welcome for every one of us."

And for to maken you the moré merry
I will myselfen goodly with you ride   *gladly*
Right at mine owné cost, and be your guide.

They all accept, proposing that the Host be MC, and then they go to bed.

This thing was granted and our oathés swore
With full glad heart, and prayéd him also
That he would vouchésafe for to do so   *agree*
And that he wouldé be our governor
And of our talés judge and reporter,
And set a supper at a certain price,
And we will ruléd be at his device   *direction*
And thereupon the wine was fetched anon.
820   We dranken, and to resté went each one
Withouten any longer tarrying.

*The next morning they set out and draw lots to see
who shall tell the first tale.*

A-morrow, when the day began to spring
Up rose our Host, and was our aller cock,[1]
And gathered us together in a flock,
And forth we rode a little more than pace   *no great speed*
Unto the watering of St Thomas.[2]
And there our Host began his horse arrest,   *halt*
And said: "Lords, hearkeneth if you lest.   *Listen, if you please*
Let see now who shall tell the firsté tale.   *Let's see*
As ever may I drinken wine or ale,
Whoso be rebel to my judgément   *Whoever is*
Shall pay for all that by the way is spent.

835   Now drawéth cut, ere that we further twinn;   *draw lots before we go*
He which that has the shortest shall begin.
Sir Knight," quod he, "my master and my lord,   *said he*
Now draweth cut, for that is mine accord.   *draw lots / wish*

---

[1] 823: "He was the cock (rooster) for all of us." That is, he got us all up
at cockcrow.

[2] 826: This is obviously the first watering place for the horses.

Come near," quod he, "my lady Prioress.
And you, Sir Clerk, let be your shamefastness,   *shyness*
Nor study not. Lay hand to, every man."

Anon to drawen every wight began   *person*
And shortly for to tellen as it was,
Were it by áventure or sort or cas,   *Whether by fate, luck or fortune*
The sooth is this, the cut fell to the knight,   *The truth / the lot*
And when this good man saw that it was so,
He saidé: "Since I shall begin the game,
What! welcome be the cut, in God's name.
855   Now let us ride, and hearken what I say."
And with that word we riden forth our way
And he began with right a merry cheer   *with great good humor*
His tale anon, and said as you may hear.   *at once*

The tale of the Knight is not included in this selection of Tales.
We pass directly to the portrait and tale of the Miller.

THE MILLER AND HIS TALE

The Miller's Portrait from the General Prologue

The MILLER was a stout carl for the nones.	*strong fellow indeed*
Full big he was of brawn and eke of bones	*and also*
That provèd well, for over all there he came	*for, wherever*
At wrestling he would have always the ram.	*prize*
He was short-shouldered, broad, a thickè knarre.	*rugged fellow*
550 There was no door that he n'ould heave off harre[1]	*the hinge*
Or break it at a running with his head.	
His beard as any sow or fox was red,	
And thereto broad as though it were a spade.	*And also*
Upon the copright of his nose he had	*tip*
555 A wart, and thereon stood a tuft of hairs	
Red as the bristles of a sowè's ears.	*pig's*
His nosèthirlès blackè were and wide.	*nostrils*
A sword and buckler bore he by his side.	*shield*
His mouth as great was as a great furnace.	
560 He was a jangler and a goliardese	*loud talker & joker*
And that was most of sin and harlotries.	*& dirty talk*
Well could he stealen corn and tollèn thrice,	*take triple toll*
And yet he had a thumb of gold pardee.[2]	*by God*
A white coat and a blue hood wearèd he.	
565 A bagpipe well could he blow and sound	
And therewithal he brought us out of town.	*And with that*

---

[1] 550: "There was no door that he could not heave off its hinges."

[2] 563: A phrase hard to explain. It is sometimes said to allude to a saying that an honest miller had a thumb of gold, i.e. there is no such thing as an honest miller. But the phrase "And yet" after the information that the miller is a thief, would seem to preclude that meaning, or another that has been suggested: his thumb, held on the weighing scale, produced gold.

THE MILLER'S TALE

Introduction

The Miller's Tale is the second of *The Canterbury Tales* coming immediately after *The Knight's Tale* which it seems to parody, and before *The Reeve's Tale* which it provokes. This kind of interaction between tales and tellers is one of the distinguishing characteristics of Chaucer's collection that has often been commented on.

At the opening of *The Canterbury Tales* the Knight draws the lot to tell the first tale, a medieval romance which, like many others, tells of love and war. Set in a distant time and place, his story involves two aristocratic young warriors in pursuit of the same rather reluctant lady over whom they argue and fight with all the elaborate motions of medieval courtly love and chivalry. One of them dies in the fight, and the other gets the rather passive maiden as his prize.

The Miller's Tale, which immediately follows, is also about two young fellows who are rivals for one girl. But there is no exotic locale here and no aristocratic milieu. Instead we have a small English university town, where students lodge in the houses of townspeople. The girl in question is no reluctant damsel, but the young, pretty and discontented wife of an old carpenter in whose house Nicholas the student (or "clerk") lodges. There is plenty of competition here too, but the love talking is more country than courtly; the only battle is an uproarious exchange of hot air and hot plowshare, and the principal cheeks kissed are not on the face. Chaucer deliberately makes this wonderfully farcical tale follow immediately upon the Knight's long, elegant story of aristocratic battle and romance, which he has just shown he can write so well, even if he writes it aslant. He is, perhaps, implying slyly that the titled people, the exotic locale, and the chivalric jousting of the *The Knight's Tale* are really about much the same thing as the more homely antics of the boyos and housewives of Oxford.

The Miller's Tale is one of the great short stories in the English language and one of the earliest. It is a fabliau, that is, a short merry tale, generally about people in absurd and amusing circumstances, often naughty sexual predicaments. The stories frequently involve a betrayed husband (the cuckold), his unfaithful wife, and a cleric who is the wife's lover. Such tales were very popular in France (hence the French term *fabliau*, pl. *fabliaux*).

The Miller calls his story a "legend and a life / Both of a carpenter and of his wife" (3141-2). *Legend* and *life* both normally imply pious narratives, as in *The Golden Legend*, a famous collection of lives of the saints. The Miller's story is not going to be a pious tale about the most famous carpenter in Christian history, Joseph, or his even more famous wife, Mary the mother of Christ. So there is a touch of blasphemy about the Miller's phrase, especially as the mention of the triangle of man, wife and clerk indicates that the story is going to be a fabliau. None of the pilgims is bothered by this except the Reeve, who had been a carpenter in his youth, according to the General Prologue. His remonstration seems to be personally rather than theologically motivated.

If you have read many French tales in a collection like that by R. Hellman and R. O'Gorman, *Fabliaux* (N.Y., 1965), you will concede that Chaucer has raised this kind of yarn-telling to an art that most of the French stories do not attain or even aspire to. In most simple fabliaux names rarely matter, and the plot always goes thus: "There was this man who lived with his wife in a town, and there was this priest..." Characters are indistinguishable from each other shortly after you have read a few fabliaux.

By contrast the characters in *The Miller's Tale*—Absalom, Alison, John and Nicholas—are very memorable, and the plot is deliciously intricate and drawn out to an absurd and unnecessary complexity which is part of the joke. Even after many readings the end still manages to surprise. These and other characters who figure in Chaucer's elaborate plots have local habitations; they have names (often pretty distinctive names like Damian or Absalom); they have personalities, and sometimes talk in quite distinctive ways, like the students with northern accents in *The Reeve's Tale*.

There is no regional accent here, but Absalom's language when he is wooing Alison (3698-3707) is a quaint mixture of the exotically Biblical, which goes with his name, and the quaintly countrified, which goes with his home. He mixes scraps of the biblical *Song of Songs* with mundane details of life in a small town. Alison's response reverses the expected sexual roles; where he is dainty, she is blunt, not so much *daungerous* as dangerous, even threatening to throw stones.

In a much-used translation of the *Canterbury Tales* from the early years of this century, by Tatlock and Mackaye, *The Miller's Tale* is censored so heavily that the reader is hard put to it to tell what is going on. Custom at that time and for long afterward did not permit the bawdiness of the tale to be accepted "frankly," as we would now put it. This squeamishness was not peculiar to the late Victorian sensibility, however. Chaucer himself realized that some people of his own day (like some in ours) might well take exception to the "frank" treatment of adulterous sex. So, just before the tale proper begins, he does warn any readers of delicate sensibility who do not wish to hear ribald tales, and invites them to "turn over the leaf and choose another tale" of a different kind, for he does have some pious and moral stories.

Along with the warning to the reader comes a kind of apologetic excuse: Chaucer pretends that he was a real pilgrim on that memorable journey to Canterbury, and that he is now simply and faithfully reproducing a tale told by another real pilgrim, a miller by trade. Such fellows are often coarse, naturally, but Chaucer cannot help that, he says. If he is to do his job properly, he must reproduce the tale exactly, complete with accounts of naughty acts and churlish words. Of course, nobody has given Chaucer any such job. There is no real miller; he is totally Chaucer's creation—words, warts and all. Drunken medieval millers did not speak in polished couplets, and a medieval reeve who brought up the rear of a mounted procession of thirty people could not indulge in verbal sparring with someone who headed up that same procession. We are clearly dealing with fiction in spite of Chaucer's jocose attempt to excuse himself for telling entertaining indecorous tales.

Another excuse and warning: it is only a joke, he says; one "should not make earnest of game," a warning often neglected by solemn critics.

Some Further Linguistic Notes

Spelling:

Sometimes the same word occurs with and without pronounced - ė :
tubbės at line 3626, but *tubs* at 3627; *legs*, but *leggės* 3330; *dearė spouse* 3610, but *hostė lief and dear* 3501; *goodė* 3154 and *good* 3155; *sweet* 3206; *sweetė* 3219; *young* 3225, *youngė* 3233; *carpenter* occurs often, but its possessive consistently has an -ė- at the end: *carpenterė's*

y- : *y-told*, has *y-take, y-covered, y-clad*. The word means the same with and without the *y-*

-en : *withouten*, I will not *tellen*; I shall *saven*. Again the words mean the same with or without the -en

Rhymes:

sail / counsel;

Nicholas, rhymes with *alas, was, solace, case*;

likerous / mouse.

wood, blood, flood 3507-8, 3518 (See also Stress below)

Stress:

Mostly *míller*, but *millér* (3167); *certáin* to rhyme with *sayn* and *again* (3495) but *cértain* 3 times

PROLOGUE to the MILLER'S TALE

*The Host is delighted with the success of his tale-telling suggestion:
everyone agrees that the first tale, the Knight's, was a good one.*

When that the knight had thus his tale y-told,	
3110 In all the company ne was there young nor old	*there was nobody*
That he ne said it was a noble story	*that didn't say*
And worthy for to drawen to memory,	*keep in memory*
And namely the gentles every one.	*especially the gentry*
Our Hosté laughed and swore: "So may I gone!	*On my word!*
3115 This goes aright. Unbuckled is the mail.	*bag*
Let's see now who shall tell another tale,	
For truly the game is well begun.	
Now telleth you, sir Monk, if that you can,[1]	
Somewhat to quité with the Knighté's tale."	*something to match*
3120 The Miller that fordrunken was all pale	*very drunk*
So that unnethe upon his horse he sat.	*scarcely*
He n'ould avalen neither hood nor hat	*wouldn't take off*
N'abiden no man for his courtesy,	*Nor wait politely*
But in Pilaté's voice he gan to cry[2]	*a bullying voice*
3125 And swore by armés, and by blood and bones:	
"I can a noble talé for the nones	*I know / occasion*
With which I will now quit the Knighté's tale."	*requite, match*
Our Hosté saw that he was drunk of ale	
And said: "Abidé, Robin, levé brother,	*Wait / dear*
3130 Some better man shall tell us first another.	
Abide, and let us worken thriftily."	
"By Godé's soul," quod he, "that will not I,	
For I will speak, or elsé go my way."	
Our Host answered: "Tell on, a devil way.	*devil take you*

---

[1] 3118: "Telleth" (plural) is the polite form of the imperative singular here.
It means "tell."

[2] 3124: In medieval mystery or miracle plays the biblical characters of Pontius Pilate
and of Herod were always represented as ranting loudly. Though all such plays that sur-
vive come from after Chaucer's time, the tradition seems to have been already established.

3135   Thou art a fool; thy wit is overcome."
        "Now hearkeneth," quod the Miller, "all and some.   *listen / everyone*
        But first I make a protestatïon
        That I am drunk; I know it by my sound
        And therefore, if that I misspeak or say,
3140   Wit it the ale of Southwark, I you pray   *Blame*
        For I will tell a legend and a life
        Both of a carpenter and of his wife,
        How that a clerk hath set the wrightė's cap."   *fooled the worker*

The Reeve, who has been a carpenter in his youth, objects.

        The Reeve answered and saidė: "Stint thy clap.   *Stop your chatter*
3145   Let be thy lewėd, drunken harlotry.[1]
        It is a sin and eke a great folly   *and also*
        T'apeiren any man or him defame   *To slander*
        And eke to bringen wivės in such fame.   *(bad) reputation*
        Thou may'st enough of other thingės sayn."
3150   This drunken Miller spoke full soon again
        And saidė: "Levė brother Osėwald,   *Dear*
        Who has no wife, he is no cuckold,   *betrayed husband*
        But I say not therefore that thou art one.
        There be full goodė wivės — many a one,
3155   And ever a thousand good against one bad.
        That know'st thou well thyself but if thou mad.   *unless thou art mad*
        Why art thou angry with my talė now?
        I have a wife, pardee, as well as thou,   *by God*
        Yet, n'ould I for the oxen in my plough   *I would not*
3160   Take upon me morė than enough
        As deemen of myself that I were one.   *think / "one"= cuckold*
        I will believė well that I am none.
        A husband shall not be inquisitive
        Of Godė's privity, nor of his wife.   *secrets, privacy*
3165   So he may findė Godė's foison there,   *Provided / G's plenty*

---

[1] 3145 The Reeve is angry because, as a onetime carpenter, he feels the tale is going to be directed at him. He is probably right, and gets his revenge when his turn comes, by telling a tale where a miller is the butt of the joke.

Of the remnant needeth not enquire."[1]
What should I moré say, but this Millér
He n'ould his wordés for no man forbear   *wouldn't restrain*
But told his churlé's tale. In his mannér,   *vulgar story*
3170 Methinketh that I shall rehearse it here.   *I think I'll retell*

Once again the poet makes a mock apology for the tale he is going to tell:
he has to tell the story as he has heard it from this rather vulgar fellow,
a churl. Those who do not like bawdy tales are given fair warning.

And therefore, every gentle wight I pray   *well bred person*
Deem not, for Godé's lové, that I say   *Judge not*
Of evil intent, but for I must rehearse   *because I must retell*
Their talés all, be they better or worse,
3175 Or elsé falsen some of my mattér.   *falsify*
And, therefore, whoso list it not to hear   *whoever wishes*
Turn over the leaf and choose another tale,
For he shall find enough, great and small,
Of storial thing that toucheth gentleness   *of narratives / nobility*
3180 And eke morality and holiness.   *also*
Blameth not me if that you choose amiss.   *"Blameth"= Blame*
The Miller is a churl; you know well this.   *low born man*
So was the Reevé eke and others mo'   *also / more*
And harlotry they tolden bothé two.   *ribald tales*
3185 Aviseth you and put me out of blame.   *Take care*
And eke men shall not make earnest of game.[2]   *seriousness of a joke*

---

[1] 3162-6: A husband should not enquire about his wife's secrets or God's. Provided his wife gives him all the sexual satisfaction he wants (*God's foison,* i.e. God's plenty), he should not enquire into what else she may be doing.

[2] 3186: "Besides, you should not take seriously (*make earnest*) what was intended as a joke (*game*)."

THE MILLER'S TALE

An old carpenter of Oxford takes in a student as a boarder.

Whilom there was dwelling at Oxenford	*Once upon a time*
A richė gnof that guestės held to board	*fellow who kept lodgers*
And of his craft he was a carpenter.	*And by trade*
3190 With him there was dwelling a poor scholar	
Had learnėd art, but all his fantasy	*all his attention*
Was turnėd for to learn astrology;[1]	
And could a certain of conclusïons	*knew some*
To deemen by interrogatïons	*judge by observation*
3195 If that men askėd him in certain hours	
When that men should have drought or elsė showers,	
Or if men askėd him what shall befall.	
Of everything, I may not reckon them all.	

A pen portrait of Handy Nicholas, the lodger

This clerk was clepėd Handy Nicholas.[2]	*was called*
3200 Of dernė love he could and of solace[3]	
And thereto he was sly and full privy	*And also / secretive*
And like a maiden meekė for to see.	
A chamber had he in that hostelry	
Alone, withouten any company,	
3205 Full fetisly y-dight with herbės soot	*nicely strewn / sweet*
And he himself as sweet as is the root	
Of liquorice or any setėwale.	*(a spice)*
His Almagest and bookės great and small,	*His astrology text*
His astrolabė longing for his art,	*belonging to*
3210 His augrim stonės lying fair apart[4]	*algorithm stones*

---

[1] 3191-2: He had studied the Seven Liberal Arts: Grammar, Rhetoric, and Logic (the Trivium); the Quadrivium covered Arithmetic, Geometry, Music, Astrology. Then, as now, there was little money in most of these; then, as now, the most profitable was probably astrology, which then included genuine astronomy.

[2] 3199: M.E. *hende* (which I have rendered "handy") meant a variety of things, all relevant to Nicholas: close at hand; pleasant; goodlooking; clever; and, as we shall see, handy, i.e. good with his hands.

[3] 3200: "He knew about secret (*derne*) love and (sexual) pleasure (*solace*)".

[4] 3208-10: The Almagest was a standard text in astrology; an astrolabe was an instrument for calculating the position of heavenly bodies, an early sextant. Augrim (algorithm) stones were counters for use in mathematical calculations.

On shelvės couchėd at his beddė's head,   *placed*
His press y-covered with a falding red   *cupboard / red cloth*
And all above there lay a gay sautry   *fine guitar*
On which he made a-nightės melody   *at night*
3215 So sweetėly that all the chamber rang
And "Angelus ad Virginem" he sang.[1]
And after that he sang the kingė's note.
Full often blessėd was his merry throat.
And thus this sweetė clerk his timė spent
3220 After his friendės' finding and his rent.[2]

The Carpenter and his young wife

This carpenter had wedded new a wife
Which that he lovėd morė than his life.
Of 18 years she was of age.
Jealous he was and held her narrow in cage,   *cooped up*
3225 For she was wild and young and he was old
And deemed himself be like a cuckėwold.[3]
He knew not Cato, for his wit was rude,[4]   *uneducated*
That bade a man should wed his similitude.   *one like himself*
Men shouldė wedden after their estate,   *according to status*
3230 For youth and eld is often at debate,   *age / at odds*
But since that he was fallen in the snare,
He must endure, as other folk, his care.

A pen portrait of Alison, the attractive young wife of the old carpenter

Fair was this youngė wife, and therewithal   *Pretty / & also*
As any weasel her body gent and small.   *slim*
3235 A ceint she wearėd, barrėd all of silk   *belt / striped*
A barmcloth eke as white as morning milk   *apron*
Upon her lendės, full of many a gore.   *hips / pleat*

---

[1] 3216-7: "Angelus ad Virginem," the Angel to the Virgin (Mary), a religious song about the Annunciation. "King's note" (3217) has not been satisfactorily explained.

[2] 3220: Supported by his friends and with his own earnings (from astrology?).

[3] 3226: "And he thought it likely he would become a cuckold (i.e. a betrayed husband)."

[4] 3227: Cato was the name given to the author of a Latin book commonly used in medieval schools, which contained wise sayings like: People should marry partners of similar rank and age.

White was her smock and broiden all before	*embroidered*
And eke behind and on her collar about	*And also*
3240 Of coal black silk within and eke without.	
The tapės of her whitė voluper	*cap*
Were of the samė suit of her collar;	*same kind*
Her fillet broad of silk and set full high.	*headband*
And sikerly she had a likerous eye.	*seductive*
3245 Full small y-pullėd were her browės two	*well plucked*
And those were bent and black as any sloe	*arched / berry*
She was full morė blissful on to see	
Than is the newė pear-jennetting tree,	*early-ripening pear*
And softer than the wool is of a wether.	*sheep*
3250 And by her girdle hung a purse of leather	*her belt*
Tasselled with silk and pearlėd with lattoun.	*beaded with brass*
In all this world to seeken up and down	
There is no man so wisė that could thench	*imagine*
So gay a popelot or such a wench.	*So pretty a doll / girl*
3255 Full brighter was the shining of her hue	*complexion*
Than in the Tower the noble forgėd new.	*in the Mint the coin*
But of her song, it was as loud and yern	*eager*
As any swallow sitting on a barn.	
Thereto she couldė skip and make a game	*Also / & play*
3260 As any kid or calf following his dame.	*his mother*
Her mouth was sweet as bragot or the meeth	*(sweet drinks)*
Or hoard of apples laid in hay or heath.	*or heather*
Wincing she was as is a jolly colt,	*Lively*
Long as a mast and upright as a bolt.	
3265 A brooch she bore upon her lower collar	
As broad as is the boss of a buckeler.	*knob of a shield*
Her shoes were lacėd on her leggės high.	
She was a primerole, a piggy's-eye	*(names of flowers)*
For any lord to layen in his bed	
3270 Or yet for any good yeoman to wed	

Handy Nick's very direct approach to Alison

Now sir, and eft sir, so befell the case	*and again*
That on a day this Handy Nicholas	
Fell with this youngė wife to rage and play	*Began ... to flirt*
While that her husband was at Osėnay,	

3275 As clerkės be full subtle and full quaint;   *v. clever & ingenious*
And privily he caught her by the quaint   *crotch*
And said: "Y-wis, but if I have my will,   *Certainly, unless*
For dernė love of thee, lemman, I spill."[1]   *secret / darling*
And held her hardė by the haunchė bones
3280 And saidė: "Lemman, love me all at once   *sweetheart*
Or I will die, all so God me save."[2]
And she sprang as a colt does in the trave   *in the shafts*
And with her head she wriėd fast away   *twisted*
And said: "I will not kiss thee, by my fay.   *faith*
3285 Why, let be," quod she, "let be, Nicholas
Or I will cry out 'Harrow!' and 'Alas!'   *(Cries of alarm)*
Do way your handės, for your courtesy."   *for your c. = please!*
   This Nicholas gan mercy for to cry   *forgiveness*
And spoke so fair, and proffered him so fast,   *pressed her*
3290 That she her love him granted at the last.
And swore her oath by Saint Thomas of Kent
That she would be at his commandėment
When that she may her leisure well espy.   *see a good chance*
"My husband is so full of jealousy
3295 That but you waitė well and be privy,   *That unless / & be discreet*
I wot right well I n'am but dead," quod she.[3]
"You mustė be full derne as in this case."   *v. secretive*
"Nay, thereof care thee not," quod Nicholas.
"A clerk had litherly beset his while
3300 But if he could a carpenter beguile."[4]
And thus they be accorded and y-swore   *agreed & sworn*
To wait a time, as I have said before.
   When Nicholas had done thus every deal
And thwackėd her upon the lendės well,   *patted her bottom*
3305 He kissed her sweet and taketh his sautry   *guitar*
And playeth fast and maketh melody.

---

[1] 3278: "I will die (*I spill*) of suppressed (*derne*) desire for you, sweetheart (*lemman*)."

[2] 3281: "I will die, I declare to God."

[3] 3295-6: "Unless you are patient and discreet (*privy*), I know (*I wot*) well that I am as good as dead."

[4] 3299-3300: "A student would have used his time badly if he could not fool a carpenter."

Then fell it thus, that to the parish church
Of Christé's owné workés for to work
This good wife went upon a holy day.
3310 Her forehead shone as bright as any day,
So was it washéd when she let her work.   *left*

Enter another admirer, the foppish parish assistant,
Absalom or Absalon, a man of many talents

Now was there of that church a parish clerk
The which that was y-clepéd Absalon.[1]   *who was called*
Curled was his hair, and as the gold it shone,
3315 And strouted as a fan, large and broad.   *spread*
Full straight and even lay his jolly shode.   *his neat hair parting*
His rode was red, his eyen grey as goose.[2]   *complexion / eyes*
With Paulé's windows carven on his shoes.[3]   *St. Paul's*
In hosen red he went full fetisly.   *red stockings / stylishly*
3320 Y-clad he was full small and properly   *neatly*
All in a kirtle of a light waget.   *tunic of light blue*
Full fair and thické be the pointés set.   *laces*
And thereupon he had a gay surplice   *church vestment*
As white as is the blossom upon the rise.   *bough*
3325 A merry child he was, so God me save.   *lad / I declare*
Well could he letten blood, and clip and shave, *draw blood & cut hair*
And make a charter of land or aquittance.   *or quitclaim*
In twenty manner could he skip and dance   *20 varieties*
After the school of Oxenfordé tho   *In Oxford style there*
3330 And with his leggés casten to and fro   *kick*
And playen songs upon a small ribible.   *fiddle*

---

[1] 3312-13: This clerk — the town dandy, surgeon barber and lay lawyer — is not a student nor a priest but a lay assistant to the pastor of the parish. Absalom or Absolon was an unusual name for an Englishman in the 14th century. The biblical Absalom was a byword for male, somewhat effeminate beauty, especially of his hair: "In all Israel there was none so much praised as Absalom for his beauty. And when he polled his head... he weighed the hair at two hundred shekels." (II Sam. 14:25-6).

[2] 3317: "He had a pink complexion and goose-grey eyes." Goose-grey or glass-grey eyes were generally reserved for heroines of romances.

[3] 3318: A design cut into the shoe leather which resembled the windows of St Paul's cathedral, the height of fashion, presumably.

Thereto he sang sometimes a loud quinible   *Also / treble*
And as well could he play on a gitern.   *guitar*
In all the town n'as brewhouse nor tavern   *there wasn't*
3335   That he ne visited with his solace   *entertainment*
Where any gaillard tapster was.   *pretty barmaid*
But sooth to say, he was somedeal squeamish
Of farting, and of speechė daungerous.   *fastidious*

Absalom notices Alison in church

This Absalom that jolly was and gay   *& well dressed*
3340   Goes with a censer on the holy day   *incense burner*
Censing the wivės of the parish fast,[1]
And many a lovely look on them he cast
And namely on this carpenterė's wife.   *especially*
To look on her him thought a merry life.   *seemed to him*
3345   She was so proper and sweet and likerous,   *pretty / seductive*
I dare well say, if she had been a mouse
And he a cat, he would her hent anon.   *seize her at once*
This parish clerk, this jolly Absalon,
Hath in his heartė such a love longing
3350   That of no wife ne took he no offering.
For courtesy, he said, he wouldė none.   *would (take)*

Absalom serenades Alison

The moon when it was night, full brightė shone
And Absalom his gitern has y-take   *guitar*
For paramours he thoughtė for to wake;[2]
3355   And forth he goes, jolly and amorous,
Till he came to the carpenterė's house
A little after the cockės had y-crow,   *had crowed*
And dressed him up by a shot window[3]
That was upon the carpenterė's wall.

---

[1] 3341: It was the custom at one or more points in the service for the clerk or altarboy to turn to the congregation swinging the incense (*censing*) several times in their direction as a gesture of respect and blessing.

[2] 3354: Either "For love's sake he intended to stay awake" or "For lovers he intended to serenade."

[3] 3358: "Took up his position near a shuttered window."

3360	He singeth in his voice gentle and small:	
	"Now, dearė lady, if thy willė be,[1]	
	I pray you that you will rue on me,"	*have pity*
	Full well accordant to his giterning.	*w. guitar accompaniment*
	This carpenter awoke and heard him sing	
3365	And spoke unto his wife and said anon:	
	"What, Alison, hear'st thou not Absalon	
	That chanteth thus under our bower's wall?"	*bedroom*
	"Yes, God wot, John. I hear it every deal."	

Absalom courts her by every means he can

3370	This passeth forth. What will you bet than well?[2]	
	From day to day this jolly Absalon	
	So wooeth her that he is woe-begone.	
	He waketh all the night and all the day,	*He stays awake*
	He combed his lockės broad and made him gay.	*& dressed up*
3375	He wooeth her by means and by brocage	*by proxies & agents*
	And swore he wouldė be her ownė page.	*servant boy*
	He singeth, brocking as a nightingale.	*trilling*
	He sent her piment, mead and spicėd ale	*flavored wine*
	And wafers piping hot out of the gleed	*out of the fire*
3380	And for she was of town, he proffered meed;	*And because / money*
	For some folk will be wonnė for richesse	*won by riches*
	And some for strokes, and some for gentleness.	*by beating*
	Sometimes to show his lightness and mastery	*agility & skill*
	He playeth Herodės upon a scaffold high.[3]	*stage*

Absalom's wooing is in vain: she loves Handy Nick

3385	But what availeth him as in this case?	
	So loveth she this Handy Nicholas	
	That Absalom may blow the buckė's horn.	*whistle in wind*
	He ne had for his labor but a scorn.	*had not*

---

[1] 3361: Addressing a carpenter's wife as "lady" was far more flattering in the 14th century than it would be now.

[2] 3370: "This went on. What can I say?"

[3] 3384: Absalom seems rather miscast as Herod in a mystery play. Herod, like Pilate, is always portrayed as a tyrant in such plays, and he rants, roars and threatens. His voice is never "gentle and small." Hence Hamlet's later complaint about ham actors who "out-herod Herod." See 3124 above.

And thus she maketh Absalom her ape
3390 And all his earnest turneth to a jape. *joke*
Full sooth is this provérb, it is no lie, *v. true*
Men say right thus: "Always the nighé sly *near sly one*
Maketh the farré leevé to be loth."[1] *farther beloved / hated*
For though that Absalom be wood or wroth, *mad or angry*
3395 Because that he was farré from her sight *farther*
This nighé Nicholas stood in his light. *closer N.*
Now bear thee well, thou Handy Nicholas, *be happy*
For Absalom may wail and sing "Alas!"

*Nicholas concocts an elaborate plan
so that he can make love to Alison*

And so befell it on a Saturday
3400 This carpenter was gone to Osénay
And Handy Nicholas and Alison
Accorded been to this conclusïon: *Have agreed*
That Nicholas shall shapen them a wile *devise a trick*
This silly jealous husband to beguile, *to deceive*
3405 And if so be this gamé went aright,
She shouldé sleepen in his arms all night,
For this was her desire and his also.
And right anon withouten wordés mo' *more*
This Nicholas no longer would he tarry
3410 But doth full soft unto his chamber carry
Both meat and drinké for a day or tway, *Both food & / two*
And to her husband bade her for to say
If that he askéd after Nicholas,
She shouldé say she n'isté where he was; *did not know*
3415 Of all that day she saw him not with eye.
She trowéd that he was in malady, *She guessed / sick*
For, for no cry her maiden could him call. *maid*
He n'ould answer, for nothing that might fall. *would not / happen*
This passeth forth all thilké Saturday *all that*
3420 That Nicholas still in his chamber lay
And ate and slept or didé what him lest *did w. pleased him*
Till Sunday that the sunné goes to rest. *sun*

---

[1] 3392-3: "The sly one who is nearby (*nighé*) causes the more distant beloved (*the farré levé*) to become unloved." i.e. Absence makes the heart grow farther.

The carpenter, worried about Nick's absence,
sends a servant up to enquire

This silly carpenter has great marvel
Of Nicholas or what thing might him ail,
3425   And said: "I am adread, by St. Thomás,
It standeth not aright with Nicholas.
God shieldé that he died suddenly.   *God forbid*
This world is now full tickle sikerly.   *unsure certainly*
I saw today a corpsé borne to church
3430   That now on Monday last I saw him work."
"Go up," quod he unto his knave anon.   *servant lad, then*
"Clepe at his door, or knocké with a stone.   *Call*
Look how it is and tell me boldély."
This knavé goes him up full sturdily.
3435   And at the chamber door while that he stood,
He cried and knockéd as that he were wood: *mad*
"What! How? What do you, Master Nicholay?
How may you sleepen all the longé day?"
But all for nought; he heardé not a word.
3440   A hole he found full low upon a board   *he = boy*
There as the cat was wont in for to creep,   *was accustomed*
And at that hole he lookéd in full deep
And at the last he had of him a sight.
This Nicholas sat ever gaping upright
3445   As he had kikéd on the newé moon.   *gaped*
Adown he goes and told his master soon
In what array he saw this ilké man.   *condition / this same*

The carpenter shakes his head at the
excessive curiosity of intellectuals.
He is glad that he is just a simple working man

This carpenter to blessen him began   *bless himself*
And said: "Help us, St. Fridéswide.   *(an Oxford saint)*
3450   A man wot little what shall him betide.   *knows / happen*
This man is fall, with his astronomy,
In some woodness or in some agony.   *madness / fit*
I thought aye well how that it shouldé be.   *I always knew*
Men should not know of Godé's privity.   *secrets*

3455	Yea, blessèd be always a lewèd man	*an illiterate man*
	That nought but only his beliefè can.[1]	
	So fared another clerk with astromy.	*astronomy*
	He walkèd in the fieldès for to pry	
	Upon the stars, what there should befall—	
3460	Till he was in a marlèpit y-fall.	*claypit*
	He saw not that. But yet, by St. Thomás,	
	Me reweth sore of Handy Nicholas.	*It grieves me*
	He shall be rated of his studying,	*rebuked for*
	If that I may, by Jesus, heaven's king.	

*With Robin's help he breaks down
the door to Nick's room*

3465	Get me a staff, that I may underspore,	*lever up*
	Whilst that thou, Robin, heavest up the door.	
	He shall out of his studying, as I guess."	
	And to the chamber door he gan him dress.	*he applied himself*
	His knavè was a strong carl for the nonce	*strong fellow indeed*
3470	And by the hasp he heaved it up at once.	
	On to the floor the doorè fell anon.	
	This Nicholas sat aye as still as stone	*stayed sitting*
	And ever gapèd up into the air.	
	This carpenter wend he were in despair[2]	*thought he was*
3475	And hent him by the shoulder mightily	*seized*
	And shook him hard and crièd spitously:	*vehemently*
	"What Nicholay! What how! What! Look adown.	
	Awake and think on Christè's passïon.	
	I crouchè thee from elvès and from wights."	*I bless / (evil) creatures*
3480	Therewith the night-spell said he anonrights[3]	
	On fourè halvès of the house about	*sides*
	And on the threshold of the door without.	

---

[1] 3455-6: "Blessed is the illiterate man who knows (*can*) nothing but his belief [in God]."

[2] 3474: The carpenter's fine theological judgement diagnoses the symptoms as those of someone who has succumbed to one of the two sins against the virtue of Hope, namely Despair. He is wrong; Nicholas's defect is the other sin against Hope—Presumption.

[3] 3479-80: "'I make the sign of the cross [to protect] you from elves and [evil] creatures.' Then he said the night prayer at once."

"Jesus Christ, and Saintė Benedict
Bless this house from every wicked wight,
3485 For the night's verie, the whitė Pater Noster.
Where wentest thou, Saintė Peter's soster?"[1]   *sister*

> *Nicholas finally pretends to come to, and promises*
> *to tell the carpenter a secret in strictest confidence*

And at the last, this Handy Nicholas
Gan for to sighė sore and said: "Alas!
Shall all the world be lost eftsoonės now?"   *right now*
3490 This carpenter answered: "What sayest thou?
What, think on God, as we do, men that swink."   *work*
This Nicholas answered: "Fetch me drink.
And after will I speak in privity   *privacy*
Of certain things that toucheth me and thee.   *concern me*
3495 I will tell it to no other man, certáin."
This carpenter goes down and comes again
And brought of mighty ale a largė quart
And when that each of them had drunk his part
This Nicholas his doorė fastė shut
3500 And down the carpenter by him he sat
And saidė: "John, my hostė lief and dear,   *lief = beloved*
Thou shalt upon thy truth swear to me here
That to no wight thou shall this counsel wray,   *no person / divulge*
For it is Christė's counsel that I say,
3505 And if thou tell it man, thou art forlore,   *man=anyone / lost*
For this vengeancė shalt thou have therefore
That if thou wrayė me, thou shalt be wood."   *betray me / go mad*
"Nay, Christ forbid it for his holy blood,"
Quod then this silly man. "I am no labb.   *blabber*
3510 And though I say, I am not lief to gab.   *not fond of gabbing*
Say what thou wilt. I shall it never tell
To child nor wife, by Him that harrowed Hell."[2]   *i.e. by Christ*

---

[1] 3483-6: The third and fourth lines of this "prayer" are pious gobbledygook of the carpenter's creation, a version of some prayer he has heard or rather misheard. *Pater Noster* is Latin for *Our Father*, the Lord's Prayer, but *white P.N.* is obscure, as is *verie. Soster* for the more usual *suster* may be an attempt at dialect usage.

[2] 3512: A favorite medieval legend told how Christ, in the interval between His death on the cross and His resurrection, went to Hell (or Limbo) to rescue from Satan's power the Old Testament heroes and heroines from Adam and Eve onwards. This was the Harrowing of Hell.

There is going to be a new Deluge like the biblical one, but Nicholas can
save only the carpenter and his wife — IF John does as he is told

"Now, John," quod Nicholas, "I will not lie.
I have found in my astrology
3515   As I have lookèd on the moonè bright
That now on Monday next, at quarter night   *about 9 p.m.*
Shall fall a rain, and that so wild and wood   *furious*
That half so great was never Noah's flood.
This world," he said, "in lessè than an hour
3520   Shall all be drenched, so hideous is the shower.   *drowned*
Thus shall mankindè drench and lose their life."
This carpenter answered: "Alas, my wife!
And shall she drench? Alas, my Alison!"
For sorrow of this he fell almost adown
3525   And said: "Is there no remedy in this case?"
"Why, yes, 'fore God," quod Handy Nicholas,   *before God*
"If thou wilt worken after lore and redde.[1]   *by advice & counsel*
Thou mayst not worken after thine own head.
For thus says Solomon that was full true:
3530   'Work all by counsel and thou shalt not rue.'   *by advice / regret*
And if thou worken wilt by good counsel,
I undertake, withouten mast or sail,
Yet shall I saven her and thee and me.
Hast thou not heard how savèd was Noë   *Noah*
3535   When that Our Lord had warnèd him before
That all the world with water should be lore?"   *lost*
"Yes," quod this carpenter, "full yore ago."   *long ago*

Nicholas gives John instructions on how to prepare for the Flood

"Hast thou not heard," quod Nicholas, "also
The sorrow of Noah with his fellowship   *and his family*
3540   Ere that he mightè get his wife to ship?   *Before he could*
Him had lever, I dare well undertake,   *He'd rather / I bet*
At thilkè time, than all his wethers black,   *At that time / sheep*

---

[1] 3527: "If you will follow advice and counsel."

That she had had a ship herself alone.[1]   *to herself*
And therefore, wost thou what is best to done?   *know you?/ to do*
3545   This asketh haste, and of a hasty thing
       Men may not preach or maken tarrying.   *or delay*
       Anon, go get us fast into this inn   *Quickly / house*
       A kneading trough or else a kimelin   *tub*
       For each of us; but look that they be large
3550   In which we mayen swim as in a barge.
       And have therein victuals sufficient   *food enough*
       But for a day. Fie on the remnant!   *Never mind the rest!*
       The water shall aslake and go away   *slacken off*
       Aboutė prime upon the nextė day.   *About 9 a.m.*
3555   But Robin may not wit of this, thy knave,   *not know / servant*
       Nor eke thy maiden Gill I may not save.
       Askė not why, for though thou askė me
       I will not tellen Godė's privity.   *secrets*
       Sufficeth thee, but if thy wittės mad,   *unless you're mad*
3560   To have as great a grace as Noah had.
       Thy wife shall I well saven, out of doubt.
       Go now thy way, and speed thee hereabout.   *busy yourself*
       But when thou hast for her and thee and me
       Y-gotten us these kneading tubbės three,   *tubs*
3565   Then shalt thou hang them in the roof full high,
       That no man of our purveyance espy.   *preparations*
       And when thou thus hast done as I have said
       And hast our victuals fair in them y-laid   *our supplies*
       And eke an axe to smite the cord a-two,   *And also / cut in two*
3570   When that the water comes, that we may go
       And break a hole on high upon the gable
       Unto the garden-ward, over the stable
       That we may freely passen forth our way
       When that the greatė shower is gone away —
3575   Then shalt thou swim as merry, I undertake,
       As does the whitė duck after her drake.

---

[1] 3538 ff: A favorite character in medieval miracle plays was "Mrs Noah" who stubbornly refuses to leave her cronies and her bottle of wine to go aboard the ark. She has to be dragged to the ark, and she boxes Noah's ears for his pains. She is the quintessential shrew. Hence the idea that Noah would have given all his prize sheep if she could have had a ship to herself.

Then will I clepe: "How, Alison! How, John!   *I will call*
Be merry, for the flood will pass anon."   *soon*
And thou wilt say: "Hail, Master Nicholay.
3580   Good morrow. I see thee well, for it is day."
And then shall we be lordès all our life
Of all the world, as Noah and his wife.

Further instructions on how to behave on the night of the Flood

But of one thing I warnè thee full right:
Be well advisèd on that ilkè night   *that same*
3585   That we be entered into shippè's board
That none of us ne speakè not a word
Nor clepe nor cry, but be in his prayer   *call out*
For it is Godè's ownè hestè dear.   *solemn order*
Thy wife and thou must hangè far a-twin   *asunder*
3590   For that betwixtè you shall be no sin,
No more in looking than there shall in deed.
This ordinance is said. Go, God thee speed.   *This order is given*
Tomorrow at night, when men be all asleep,
Into our kneading tubbès will we creep
3595   And sitten there, abiding Godè's grace.   *awaiting*
Go now thy way, I have no longer space
To make of this no longer sermoning.
Men say thus: 'Send the wise and say nothing.'
Thou art so wise, it needeth thee not teach.
3600   Go, save our lives, and that I thee beseech."

*John tells the plans to his wife (who already knows). He installs the big
tubs on the house roof, and supplies them with food and drink.*

This silly carpenter goes forth his way.
Full oft he said: "Alas!" and "Welaway!"   *(cries of dismay)*
And to his wife he told his privity
And she was 'ware and knew it bet than he   *aware / better*
3605   That all this quaintè cast was for to say.   *elaborate plot*
But natheless, she fared as she would die,   *she acted*
And said "Alas! Go forth thy way anon.
Help us to 'scape, or we be dead each one.
I am thy truè, very, wedded wife.   *thy loyal, faithful*

3610	Go, dearè spouse, and help to save our life."
	Lo, which a great thing is affectïon.	*See what / feeling*
	Men may die of imaginatïon,
	So deepè may impressïon be take.	*be made*
	This silly carpenter beginneth quake.	*shake*
3615	Him thinketh verily that he may see
	Noah's flood come wallowing as the sea
	To drenchen Alison, his honey dear.	*To drown*
	He weepeth, waileth, maketh sorry cheer.
	He sigheth, with full many a sorry swough.	*sigh*
3620	He goes and getteth him a kneading trough,
	And after that a tub and kimelin,	*vat*
	And privily he sent them to his inn	*secretly / house*
	And hung them in the roof in privity.	*in secrecy*
	His ownè hand, he madè ladders three	*(With) his own*
3625	To climben by the rungès and the stalks	*rungs & uprights*
	Unto the tubbès hanging in the balks,	*rafters*
	And them he victualled, bothè trough and tub,	*he supplied*
	With bread and cheese and good ale in a jub	*jug*
	Sufficing right enough as for a day.
3630	But ere that he had made all this array,	*before / ready*
	He sent his knave and eke his wench also	*servant boy & girl*
	Upon his need to London for to go.	*On his business*

*On the fateful night all three get into their
separate tubs, and say their prayers*

	And on the Monday, when it drew to night,
	He shut his door withouten candle light,
3635	And dressèd allè thing as it should be.	*prepared everything*
	And shortly up they clomben allè three.	*climbed*
	They sitten stillè, well a furlong way.[1]	*few minutes*
	"Now, Pater Noster, clum," said Nicholay.	*Our Father,*
	And "Clum," quod John, and "Clum," said Alison.[2]

---

[1] 3637: A "furlong way" is the time it takes to walk a furlong (1/8 of a mile)—about 2 or 3 minutes.

[2] 3638-9: "Pater Noster": the first words of the Latin version of the Lord's Prayer: Our Father. The "Clum" is meaningless, possibly a corrupt version of the end of "in saecula saeculorum," a common ending for prayers. Thus the whole prayer is ignorantly (and irreverently) reduced to beginning and ending formulas.

3640 This carpenter said his devotion
And still he sits and biddeth his prayer   *offers*
Awaiting on the rain if he it hear.
The deadė sleep, for weary busy-ness,
Fell on this carpenter, right (as I guess)
3645 Aboutė curfew time or little more.   *About nightfall*
For travailing of his ghost he groaneth sore   *In agony of spirit*
And eft he routeth, for his head mislay.   *also he snored*

This is the moment that Nicholas and Alison
have been waiting and planning for

Down off the ladder stalketh Nicholay   *slips*
And Alison full soft adown she sped.
3650 Withouten wordės more, they go to bed
There as the carpenter is wont to lie.   *is accustomed*
There was the revel and the melody.
And thus lie Alison and Nicholas
In busyness of mirth and of soláce   *enjoyment*
3655 Till that the bell of laudės gan to ring   *bell for morning service*
And friars in the chancel gan to sing.   *in the church*

Absalom, thinking that the carpenter is absent, comes serenading again

This parish clerk, this amorous Absalon,
That is for love always so woe-begone,
Upon the Monday was at Oseney
3660 With company, him to disport and play,
And askėd upon case a cloisterer   *by chance a monk*
Full privily after John the carpenter,   *V. quietly about*
And he drew him apart out of the church.
And said: "I n'ot; I saw him here not work   *I don't know*
3665 Since Saturday; I trow that he be went   *I guess he's gone*
For timber, there our abbot has him sent.
For he is wont for timber for to go
And dwellen at the grange a day or two;   *at outlying farm*
Or elsė he is at his house certáin.
3670 Where that he be I cannot soothly sayn."
This Absalom full jolly was and light
And thoughtė: "Now is time to wake all night,

For sikerly I saw him not stirring   *certainly*
About his door, since day began to spring.
3675   So may I thrive, I shall at cocke's crow   *On my word!*
Full privily knocken at his window
That stands full low upon his bower's wall.   *bedroom wall*
To Alison now will I tellen all
My love longing, for yet I shall not miss
3680   That at the leaste way I shall her kiss.
Some manner comfort shall I have parfay.   *in faith*
My mouth has itched all this longe day.
That is a sign of kissing at the least.
All night me mette eke I was at a feast.   *I dreamed also*
3685   Therefore I will go sleep an hour or tway,   *two*
And all the night then will I wake and play."   *& have fun*
       When that the firste cock has crowed anon
Up rist this jolly lover, Absalon   *riseth*
And him arrayeth gay at point devise.[1]
3690   But first he cheweth grain and liquorice   *cardamom*
To smellen sweet. Ere he had combed his hair,
Under his tongue a truelove he bare,   *spice he put*
For thereby wend he to be gracious.   *hoped to be attractive*
He roameth to the carpentere's house
3695   And he stands still under the shot window.   *shuttered*
Unto his breast it rought, it was so low,   *reached*
And soft he cougheth with a semi-sound.   *gentle sound*
       "What do you, honeycomb, sweet Alison?
My faire bird, my sweete cinnamon,
3700   Awaketh, lemman mine, and speak to me.   *my lover*
Well little thinken you upon my woe
That for your love I sweate there I go.   *wherever*
No wonder is though that I swelt and sweat.   *faint*
I mourn as does the lamb after the teat.
3705   Ywis, lemman, I have such love longing   *Indeed, dear*
That like a turtle true is my mourning.   *turtle-dove*
I may not eat no more than a maid."

---

[1] 3689: "Dresses himself to the nines in all his finery."

Alison's ungracious verbal response

"Go from the window, Jackė Fool," she said.
"As help me God, it will not be 'Compame'.   *'Come kiss me'(?)*
3710   I love another (or else I were to blame)
Well bet than thee, by Jesus, Absalon.   *better*
Go forth thy way, or I will cast a stone,
And let me sleep, a twenty devil way."[1]
"Alas!" quod Absalom, "and Welaway!
3715   That truė love was e'er so evil beset.[2]   *so badly treated*
Then, kiss me, since that it may be no bet,   *better*
For Jesus' love, and for the love of me."
"Wilt thou then go thy way therewith?" quod she.
"Yea, certės, lemman," quod this Absalon.   *certainly, darling*
3720   "Then make thee ready," quod she. "I come anon."

Her even **more** ungracious practical joke

And unto Nicholas she saidė still: *quietly*
"Now hush, and thou shalt laughen all thy fill."
This Absalom down set him on his knees
And said: "I am a lord at all degrees.   *in every way*
3725   For after this I hope there cometh more.
Lemman, thy grace and, sweetė bird, thine ore"[3]
The window she undoes, and that in haste.
"Have done," quod she. "Come off and speed thee fast,
Lest that our neighėbourės thee espy."
3730   This Absalom gan wipe his mouth full dry.
Dark was the night as pitch or as the coal
And at the window out she put her hole.
And Absalom, him fell nor bet nor worse,   *befell / better*
But with his mouth he kissed her naked arse
3735   Full savorly, ere he was 'ware of this.   *aware*
Aback he starts, and thought it was amiss,
For well he wist a woman has no beard.   *well he knew*
He felt a thing all rough and long y-haired

---

[1] 3713: "The devil take you twenty times"

[2] 3715: The line might be read: "That truė love was e'er so ill beset."

[3] 3726: "Darling, [grant me] your favor, and sweet bird, [grant me] your mercy."
A line parodying the love language of romances.

And saidé: "Fie! Alas! What have I do?"
3740   "Tee hee," quod she, and clapt the window to.
And Absalom goes forth a sorry pace.   *with sad step*
"A beard! a beard!" quod Handy Nicholas.   *"beard" also=joke*
"By God's corpus, this goes fair and well."   *By God's body!*

Absalom plots revenge for his humiliation

This silly Absalom heard every deal
3745   And on his lip he gan for anger bite
And to himself he said "I shall thee 'quite."   *repay you*
Who rubbeth now? Who frotteth now his lips   *scrapes*
With dust, with sand, with straw, with cloth, with chips
But Absalom that says full oft: "Alas!
3750   My soul betake I unto Satanas,   *I'll be damned*
But me were lever than all this town," quod he,   *I had rather*
Of this despite a-wreaken for to be.   *avenged for this shame*
"Alas!" quod he "Alas! I n'ad y-blent."[1]
His hoté love is cold and all y-quenched.   *hot*
3755   For from that time that he had kissed her arse
Of paramours he setté not a curse,[2]   *lovers*
For he was healéd of his malady.
Full often paramours he gan defy   *denounce*
And wept as does a child that is y-beat.   *beaten*
3760   A softé pace he went over the street   *Quietly he went*
Unto a smith men clepen Daun Gervase   *call*
That in his forge smithéd plough harness.
He sharpens share and coulter busily.   *(plough parts)*
This Absalom knocks all easily
3765   And said: "Undo, Gervase, and that anon."   *open up*
"What? Who art thou?" "It am I, Absalon."
"What, Absalon! What, Christé's sweeté tree!   *cross*
Why risé you so rathe. Hey, ben'citee!   *so early / bless you!*
What aileth you? Some gay girl, God it wot,   *pretty girl*
3770   Has brought you thus upon the viritot.   *on the prowl(?)*
By Saint Neót, you wot well what I mean."   *you know*
This Absalom ne raughté not a bean   *did not care*
Of all his play. No word again he gave.   *jesting*

---

[1] 3753: "Alas, that I did not duck aside" (?)

[2] 3756: "Curse": The intended word may be "cress," a weed.

He haddė morė tow on his distaff[1]

3775 Than Gervase knew, and saidė: "Friend so dear,

That hot coulter in the chimney here   *hot plough part*

As lend it me. I have therewith to do.   *need of it*

And I will bring it thee again full soon.

Gervasė answered: "Certės, were it gold   *Certainly*

3780 Or in a pokė nobles all untold,[2]   *bag coins uncounted*

Thou shouldst it have, as I am truė smith.

Eh! Christė's foe! What will you do therewith?"   *What the devil will ...*

"Thereof," quod Absalom, " be as be may.

I shall well tell it thee another day."

3785 And caught the coulter by the coldė steel.   *cold handle*

Full soft out at the door he 'gan to steal

And went unto the carpenterė's wall.

Absalom's revenge

He cougheth first and knocketh therewithall   *also*

Upon the window, right as he did ere.   *before*

3790 This Alison answered: "Who is there

That knocketh so? I warrant it a thief."   *I'm sure it is*

"Why, nay," quod he, "God wot, my sweetė lief.   *God knows / love*

I am thine Absalom, my darling.

Of gold," quod he, "I have thee brought a ring.

3795 My mother gave it me, so God me save.

Full fine it is, and thereto well y-grave.   *engraved*

This will I given thee, if thou me kiss."

    This Nicholas was risen for to piss

And thought he would amenden all the jape.   *improve the joke*

3800 He should kiss *his* arse ere that he 'scape.   *He = Absalom*

And up the window did he hastily

And out his arse he putteth privily

Over the buttock, to the haunchė bone.

And therewith spoke this clerk, this Absalon:

3805 "Speak, sweet heart. I wot not where thou art."   *I know not*

---

[1] 3774: "He had more wool or flax on his distaff." A distaff was a stick, traditionally used by women, to make thread from raw wool or flax. The phrase appears to mean either "He had other things on his mind" or "He had other work to do."

[2] 3779-80: "Certainly, [even] if it were gold or an uncounted (*untold*) number of coins (*nobles*) in a bag (*poke*) ..."

This Nicholas anon let fly a fart
As great as it had been a thunder dint   clap
That with that stroke he was almost y-blint.   blinded
But he was ready with his iron hot
3810 And Nicholas amid the arse he smote.   he struck
Off goes the skin a handëbreadth about.
The hot coulter burnëd so his tout   backside
That for the smart he weenëd for to die.   from pain he expected
As he were wood, for woe he 'gan to cry   As if mad
3815 "Help! Water! Water! Help! for God's heart."

The carpenter re-enters the story with a crash

This carpenter out of his slumber start
And heard one cry "Water!" as he were wood.   mad
And thought "Alas! Now cometh Noah's flood."
He set him up withouten wordës mo'   more
3820 And with his ax he smote the cord a-two   cut
And down goes all—he found neither to sell
Nor bread nor ale, till he came to the cell   bottom
Upon the floor,[1] and there aswoon he lay.

Alison and Nicholas lie their way out of the predicament

Up starts her Alison, and Nicholay,
3825 And criëd "Out!" and "Harrow!" in the street.   (Cries of alarm)
The neighëbourës, bothë small and great
In runnen for to gauren on this man   to gape
That aswoon lay, bothë pale and wan.
For with the fall he bursten had his arm,
3830 But stand he must unto his ownë harm,[2]
For when he spoke, he was anon bore down   talked down
With Handy Nicholas and Alison.   "With" = "By"
They tolden every man that he was wood;   mad
He was aghastë so of Noah's flood
3835 Through fantasy, that of his vanity

---

[1] 3821-3: "He found....floor": there was nothing between him and the
ground below.

[2] 3830: A difficult line meaning, perhaps, "He had to take the responsibility
for his injury (or misfortune)" or "He had to take the blame."

He had y-bought him kneading tubbės three[1]
And had them hangėd in the roof above
And that he prayėd them for Godė's love
To sitten in the roof "par compagnie."   *for company*
3840 The folk gan laughen at his fantasy.
Into the roof they kiken and they gape   *stare*
And turnėd all his harm into a jape   *joke*
For whatso that this carpenter answered
It was for naught. No man his reason heard.
3845 With oathės great he was so sworn adown
That he was holden wood in all the town.   *held to be mad*
For every clerk anon right held with other.[2]
They said: "The man was wood, my levė brother." *mad, my dear b.*
And every wight gan laughen at this strife.   *person*

The "moral" of the story

3850 Thus swivėd was the carpenterė's wife   *laid*
For all his keeping and his jealousy.
And Absalom has kissed her nether eye   *lower*
And Nicholas is scalded in the tout.   *on the bottom*
This tale is done, and God save all the rout.   *this group*

---

[1] 3834-6: "He was so afraid of Noah's flood in his mind that in his foolishness he had bought ...."

[2] 3847: Presumably a reference to the "town" versus "gown" loyalties in university towns. Nicholas, a "clerk," is a member of the "gown," John the carpenter a member of the "town."

THE WIFE OF BATH, HER PROLOGUE AND HER TALE

In the Wife of Bath we have one of only three women on the pilgrimage. Unlike the other two she is not a nun, but a much-married woman, a widow yet again. Everything about her is exaggerated.

The Portrait of the Wife from the General Prologue

A good WIFE was there of besidė Bath	*near*
But she was somedeal deaf, and that was scath.	*somewhat / a pity*
Her coverchiefs full finė were of ground;	*finely woven*
I durstė swear they weighėden ten pound	*dare*
That on a Sunday were upon her head.	
Her hosen weren of fine scarlet red	*stockings*
Full straight y-tied, and shoes full moist and new.	*supple*
Bold was her face and fair and red of hue.	*color*

Her Love Life

	She was a worthy woman all her life.	
460	Husbands at churchė door she had had five,[1]	
	Withouten other company in youth,	*Not counting*
	But thereof needeth not to speak as nouth.	*now*

Her Travels

And thrice had she been at Jerusalem.	*3 times*
She had passėd many a strangė stream.	*foreign*
At Romė she had been and at Boulogne,	

---

[1] 460: *at churchė door:* Weddings took place in the church porch, followed by Mass inside.

In Galicia at St James and at Cologne. *[famous shrines]*
She coulde much of wandering by the way.[1] *knew much*

More on her appearance

Gat-toothed was she, soothly for to say. *Gap-toothed / truly*
Upon an ambler easily she sat *slow horse*
470 Y-wimpled well,[2] and on her head a hat
As broad as is a buckler or a targe, *kinds of shield*
A foot mantle about her hippes large, *outer skirt*
And on her feet a pair of spurs sharp.
In fellowship well could she laugh and carp. *joke*
Of remedies of love she knew perchance *by experience*
For she could of that art the olde dance. *knew*

---

[1] 467: Chaucer does not explain, and the reader is probably not expected to ask, how the Wife managed to marry five husbands and take in pilgrimage as almost another occupation. Going to Jerusalem from England *three* times was an extraordinary feat in the Middle Ages. This list is, like some of those already encountered, a deliberate exaggeration, as is everything else about the Wife.

[2] 470: A wimple was a woman's cloth headgear covering the ears, the neck and the chin.

THE WIFE OF BATH'S TALE AND PROLOGUE

Introduction

We remember the Wife of Bath, not so much for her tale as for Chaucer's account of her in the General Prologue and, above all, for her own Prologue. For one thing, the tale itself is a rather unremarkable folktale with a lecture on true nobility somewhat awkwardly incorporated. The tale is meant to illustrate the contention of her prologue: that a marriage in which the woman has the mastery is the best, and the conclusion of one closely coincides with the other. The tale also seems to express covertly her desire to be young and beautiful again. It is not a poor tale, but neither is it of unforgettable force like the Pardoner's or of unforgettable humor like the Miller's. Moreover, the Prologue is about three times as long as the tale to which it is supposed to be a short introduction. If that is appropriate for anyone, it is so for Alison of Bath, about whom everything is large to the point of exaggeration: her bulk, her clothes, her mouth, the number of her marriages, the extent of her travels, her zest for sex, her love of domination, her torrential delivery. The result is a portrait of someone for whom it is difficult to find an analogy in English literature except perhaps Shakespeare's Falstaff or some of the characters of Dickens.

She is wonderful company provided one is not married to her and can contemplate from a distance the fate of the sixth husband whom she is seeking as voraciously as she did his predecessors: "Welcome the sixth, when that ever he shall." Shall what? Have the temerity to get too close to this medieval Venus Flytrap, and be devoured?

Oddly enough, this unforgettably ebullient figure is an amalgam of many features derived from Chaucer's reading. Many of the traits he attributes to her are essentially borrowed from that favorite of the Middle Ages, the long French poem *The Romance of the Rose*. She also embodies traits in women which misogynistic Church Fathers like Jerome and Tertullian denounced in their writings. All this illustrates what wonderfully creative work can be done with old material. The medievals liked to think that their tales were not original, that they were renewed versions of old authors who had become "authorities." Here Chaucer borrows very freely, and it is interesting to observe the result. While the elements are not original but largely borrowed from a variety of sources, the final product is the unforgettably original creation that is the Wife.

The Wife has attracted attention and comment over the centuries in abundance in contrast to, say, that pleasant and attractive lady, the Prioress. One reason is the intense personal quality that emanates from the character. Take her way of referring to herself or to women in general. Whether she is holding forth in her Prologue or telling her Tale, her pronouns slip with an engaging ease from "they" to "we" to "I" or from "women" to "we" to "I" or the other way round. Her talk is intensely hers, incapable of being confused with that of anyone else. As she is telling how she always made provision for another husband if her current victim died, she loses the thread of her discourse for a second, but only for a second:

> *But now, sir, let me see what shall I sayn?*
> *Aha, I have my tale again. (585-6)*

As she is telling her folktale of the knight and the old hag, she refers to the classical story of Midas, and immediately wants to tell it:

> *Will you hear the tale? (951)*

Her Prologue is, above all, about her—her experiences of love in and out of marriage, and her right to hold forth on that subject in spite of the "authority" of clerics who know nothing about the matter. A much-married woman, she has much more "authority" on love and marriage than any celibate clerk who knows only books, and she knows how to deal with books that do not please her too. Her outpouring is a confession of sorts but without a trace of the penitent's *mea culpa,* for as she recalls with relish: "I have had my world as in my time." The only thing she regrets is that age "Hath me bereft my beauty and my pith."

Hers is the first contribution to the Marriage Group, and it is answered in one way or another by the Tales of the Clerk, the Merchant, and the Franklin. She asks her fellow pilgrims to take it "not agrief of what I say / For my intent is not but for to play " (191-192), but the force of her polemic and her personality has attracted far more attention from readers early and late than most other characters on that famous pilgrimage.

THE WIFE OF BATH'S PROLOGUE

The Wife's narrative opens with a defense of her many marriages, all legal, as she points out, i.e. recognized by the Church even though some churchmen frowned on widows re-marrying. The Wife challenges anyone to show her where the Scripture sets a limit to the number of successive legal marriages a person can have in a lifetime. She claims that, because she has lots of experience of marriage, she is more of an authority on that subject than the celibate "authorities" who write about it. And she knows how to use "authorities" too, if it comes to it, as the many marginal references in our text show.

Experience, though no authority   *authors*
Were in this world, is right enough for me
To speak of woe that is in marrïage;[1]
For, lordings, since I twelve years was of age,[2]
5 (Thankèd be God that is etern alive)
Husbands at churchè door I have had five,
(If I so often might have wedded be).
And all were worthy men in their degree.
But me was told certain not long agone is,   *(To) me*
10 That since that Christ ne went never but once
To wedding, in the Cane of Galilee,   *John II, 1-10*
That by the same example taught he me,
That I ne shouldè wedded be but once.[3]
Lo, hark eke which a sharp word for the nonce[4]

---

[1] 1-3: "Even if no 'authorities' had written on the subject, my own experience is quite enough for me to speak with authority on the woes of marriage." By *authorities* she means the Bible, theologians and classical authors.

[2] 4: *Lordings* means something like "Ladies and gentlemen." Twelve was the legal cononical age for girls to marry. Marriages took place at the door of the church followed by mass inside.

[3] 9-13: Jerome, one of the more ascetic of the Church Fathers, suggested that because Jesus is recorded as having attended only one wedding, people should not marry more than once. The Wife scoffs at this peculiar thinking.

[4] 14-16: "Now listen also to what sharp words Jesus, who is God and man, spoke on one occasion *(for the nonce)* when he reproved the Samaritan woman at the well." In the Gospel of John (4:4-26) Jesus tells a Samaritan woman whom he meets as she is drawing water from a well, but whom he has not seen before, that she has had five husbands, and that the man she is now living with is not her husband. He does not say why her present partner is not her husband.

15   Beside a well Jesus, God and man,
      Spoke in reproof of the Samaritan: *John IV, 6-26*
      'Thou hast had fivė husbandės,' quod he;   *said he*
      'And that ilkė man which that now hath thee,   *that very man*
      Is not thy husband.' Thus he said certain;
20   What that he meant thereby, I cannot sayn.
      But that I ask why that the fifthė man
      Was no husband to the Samaritan?
      How many might she have in marrïage?
      Yet heard I never tellen in mine age   *my life*
25   Upon this number definitïon;
      Men may divine and glossen up and down.   *speculate & comment*
      But well I wot, express without a lie,   *I know / definitely*
      God bade us for to wax and multiply;   *told us to increase*
      That gentle text can I well understand.
30   Eke well I wot he said that my husband   *Also I know well*
      Should let father and mother, and take to me;   *leave (Matt. xix, 5.)*
      But of no number mentïon made he,
      Of bigamy or of octogamy;[1]   *2 or 8 marriages*
      Why should men then speak of it villainy?   *speak badly*

Holy men in the Bible had more wives than one

35   Lo, here the wisė king Daun Solomon;
      I trowė he had wivės many a one.   *I believe*
      (As would to God it lawful were to me
      To be refreshėd half so oft as he).
      Which gift of God had he for all his wivės![2]
40   No man hath such, that in this world alive is.
      God wot, this noble king, as to my wit,   *God knows / I'll wager*
      The firstė night had many a merry fit   *bout*
      With each of them, so well was him alive.   *so virile was he (?)*

---

[1] 33: "Bigamy" here means being married twice but not to two people at the same time. Later, however, the Wife seems to use the term "bigamy" in the sense of the sin or crime of bigamy (l.86). "Octogamy" = 8 marriages in a row.

[2] 39: This line means either that the gift was from God to him in granting him so many wives, or from Solomon to them, probably the former.

	Blessed be God that I have wedded five.[1]	
45	Welcome the sixthė when that ever he shall,	*shall (come along)*
	For since I will not keep me chaste in all	*totally celibate*
	When my husband is from the worldė gone,	
	Some Christian man shall weddė me anon.	
	For then, the apostle says that I am free	*Paul (I Cor VII, 9)*
50	To wed, on Godė's half, where it liketh me.	*w. God's consent / pleases me*
	He says that to be wedded is no sin;	
	Better is to be wedded than to brinne.	*burn (I, Cor VII)*
	What recketh me though folk say villainy	*What care I*
	Of shrewėd Lamech and his bigamy?[2]	*(Gen.IV, 19)*
55	I wot well Abraham was a holy man,	*I know*
	And Jacob eke, as far as ever I can,	*also / I know*
	And each of them had wivės more than two,	
	And many another holy man also.	

*Virginity is good, but is nowhere **demanded** by God*

	Where can you see in any manner age	
60	That highė God defended marrïage	*forbade*
	By express word? I pray you telleth me.	*tell me*
	Or where commanded he virginity?	
	I wot as well as you (it is no dread)	*I know / no question*
	The apostle, when he speaks of maidenhead,	*St. Paul / virginity*
65	He said that precept thereof had he none.	*command*
	Men may *counsel* a woman to be one,	*advise / be single*
	But counselling is no commandėment;	*I Cor VII, 25*
	He put it in our ownė judgėment.	
	For haddė God commanded maidenhead,	
70	Then had he damnėd wedding with the deed.	*condemned*

---

[1] 44a-44f: The following six lines do not appear in any Six Text MS, but they have been accepted by scholars as genuine Chaucer, and appear in many editions.

44a	Of which I have pickėd out the best	
	Both of their nether purse and of their chest.	*= lower purse = scrotum.*
	Divérsė schoolės maken perfect clerks	*students*
	And díverse practices in sundry works	
	Maken the workman perfect sikerly.	
44f	Of fivė husbands scholeying am I.	*I am the student*

[2] 53-4: "What do I care if people speak ill of bad Lamech and his bigamy?" Though Lamech is the first man mentioned in the Bible as taking two wives, other more famous patriarchs did also, as she points out in the following lines.

And certės, if there were no seed y-sow, *certainly / sown*
Virginity then whereof should it grow?
Paul durstė not commanden at the least *dared*
A thing of which his Master gave no hest. *no command*
75 The dart is set up for virginity, *The first prize*
Catch whoso may, who runneth best let's see.
But this word is not take of every wight, *not meant / person*
But there as God will give it of His might. *only where / power*
I wot well that the apostle was a maid, *I know / virgin*
80 But natheless, though that he wrote or said *I Cor. VII, 7*
He would that every wight were such as he, *wished t. e. person*
All n'is but counsel to virginity. *is advice only*
And for to be a wife he gave me leave
Of indulgence,[1] so n'is it no repreve *it is no reproof*
85 To weddė me, if that my makė die, *my mate*
Without exceptïon of bigamy, *accusation*
All were it good no woman for to touch, *Even if it is good...*
(He meant as in his bed or in his couch)
For peril is both fire and tow to assemble; *to join fire & flax*
90 You know what this example may resemble.
This all and some: he held virginity *In short*
More perfect than wedding in frailty: *out of*
(Frailty clepe I, but if that he and she *I call it / unless*
Would leaden all their life in chastity).
95 I grant it well, I have of none envy,[2]
Though maidenhead preferė bigamy; *is preferred over*
It likes them to be clean in body and ghost. *It pleases / b. & soul*
Of mine estate ne will I make no boast. *my state (as wife)*

Virginity is not for everyone

For well you know, a lord in his household
100 Ne has not every vessel all of gold;
Some be of tree and do their lord service. *of wood*
God clepeth folk to him in sundry wise, *G. calls / different*
And ever each has of God a proper gift, *everyone / special*

---

[1] 83-4: "He gave me leave out of indulgence (for human weakness)" or "He gave me leave to indulge."

[2] 95: "I grant that readily. I am not envious if virginity is regarded as preferable to being married more than once."

Some this, some that, as that him liketh shift.   *pleases him to choose*
105   Virginity is great perfectïon,
And continence eke with devotïon.   *And sexual restraint*
But Christ, that of perfectïon is well,   *is the source*
Bade not every wight he should go sell   *every person*
All that he had and give it to the poor,
110   And in such wisė follow him and his foor;   *fashion / steps*
He spoke to them that will live perfectly,   *wish to*
And, lordings, (by your leave) that am not I.
I will bestow the flower of all mine age
In the actės and the fruit of marrïage.

If virginity were for everyone, why do we all have sexual organs?

115   Tell me also, to what conclusïon   *for w. purpose*
Were members made of generatïon,   *sexual organs made*
And of so perfect wise a wright y-wrought?[1]
Trusteth me well, they were not made for nought.
Gloss whoso will, and say both up and down,   *Explain (away)*
120   That they were madė for purgatïon
Of urine, and our bothė thingės small[2]
Was eke to know a female from a male,
And for no other causė. Say you no?
The experience wot well it is not so.   *knows*
125   So that the clerkės be not with me wroth,   *clerics / angry*
I say this, that they makėd be for both,
This is to say, for office and for ease   *duty & pleasure*
Of engendrure, where we not God displease.   *procreation*
Why should men elsė in their bookės set
130   That man shall yield unto his wife her debt?
Now wherewith should he make his payėment,
If he ne used his silly instrument?[3]   *his blessed (?)*
Then were they made upon a creäture
To purgė urine, and eke for engendrure.   *also f. procreation*

---

[1] 117: "And made (*y-wrought*) by so perfectly wise a creator (*wright*)".

[2] 121: "Both small things". Whatever organs, male and female, the wife is thinking of, "small" is the surprising word.

[3] 132: Theologians wrote that in marriage each partner had an obligation to satisfy the other's sexual need—hence a debt that required payment when called for. This is one of the few theological teachings that appeals to the Wife, at least when she is the creditor.

Marriage is not for everyone either

135	But I say not that every wight is hold,	*person is required*
	That has such harness as I to you told,	*equipment*
	To go and usen them in engendrure;	
	Then should men take of chastity no cure.	*respect*
	Christ was a maid, and shapen as a man,	*virgin, & formed*
140	And many a saint, since that this world began,	
	Yet lived they ever in perfect chastity.	
	I n'ill envy no virginity.[1]	*will not*
	Let them be bread of purèd wheatè seed,	*refined*
	And let us wivès hotèn barley bread.	*be called*
145	And yet with barley bread, Mark tellè can,	*St. M. says*
	Our Lord Jesus refreshèd many a man.[2]	

But marriage is for Alison

	In such estate as God has clepèd us	*career / has called*
	I'll persevere; I am not precìous.	*not fastidious, snobbish*
	In wifehood will I use mine instrument	
150	As freely as my Maker has it sent.	
	If I be daungerous God give me sorrow.	*distant, frigid*
	My husband shall it have both eve and morrow,	*night and morning*
	When that him list come forth and pay his debt.	*it pleases him*
	A husband will I have, I will not let,	*I won't be stopped*
155	Which shall be both my debtor and my thrall,	*Who / my slave*
	And have his tribulatïon withall	*suffering*
	Upon his flesh while that I am his wife.	
	I have the power during all my life	
	Upon his proper body, and not he;	*his own (Fr."propre")*
160	Right thus the apostle told it unto me,	*I Cor VII, 4*
	And bade our husbands for to love us well.	*& Ephes V, 25*
	All this senténce me liketh every deal."	*t. teaching pleases me*

An interruption from an unexpected quarter

	Up starts the Pardoner, and that anon;	*suddenly*
	"Now, Dame," quod he, "by God and by Saint John,	*Now, ma'am*

---

[1] 142: As in many other places in Chaucer, the double negative is not bad grammar.

[2] 145-6: Probably a reference to the occasion where Christ miraculously multiplied a few loaves and fishes to feed a hungry multitude. See Mark 6: 38 ff

165   You be a noble preacher in this case.
        I was about to wed a wife, alas!
        What! Should I buy it on my flesh so dear?
        Yet had I lever wed no wife to-year."[1]
             "Abide," quod she, "my tale is not begun.   *Wait*
170   Nay, thou shalt drinken of another tun   *barrel*
        Ere that I go, shall savor worse than ale.   *(which) will taste*
        And when that I have told thee forth my tale
        Of tribulation in marrïage,
        Of which I am expert in all mine age,
175   (This is to say, myself has been the whip)
        Then may'st thou choose whether thou wilt sip
        Of thilkë tunnë, that I shall abroach.   *that cask / tap*
        Beware of it, ere thou too nigh approach,   *too near*
        For I shall tell examples more than ten.
180   Whoso that n'ill beware by other men   *Whoever will not*
        By him shall other men corrected be.
        These samë wordës writeth Ptolemy;   *P. the astronomer*
        Read in his Almagest, and take it there."   *A = a book on astronomy*
             "Dame, I would pray you, if your will it were,"   *Ma'am*
185   Said this Pardoner, "as you began,
        Tell forth your tale, and spareth for no man,
        And teacheth us young men of your practice."   *know-how*

"Don't take too seriously what I am going to say," she advises

        "Gladly," quod she, "since that it may you like.   *may please you*
        But that I pray to all this company,
190   If that I speak after my fantasy,   *fancy*
        As taketh not a-grief of what I say,   *offence*
        For my intent is not but for to play.
        Now, sir, then will I tell you forth my tale.
        As ever may I drinken wine or ale
195   I shall say sooth: the husbands that I had
        As three of them were good, and two were bad.
        The three men were good and rich and old.

---

[1] 166-8: "I had rather not marry this year." From the description of the Pardoner in
the General Prologue (see p. 115-117 below) it is obvious that he could never be interested
in women or marriage, a fact that leaves one free to speculate about why he should make
this remark to the Wife, whom he addresses as *Dame*, a polite, not a slang, usage.

Unnethė mighten they the statute hold   *Barely keep t. (sexual) contract*
In which that they were bounden unto me.
200 You wot well what I mean of this, pardee.   *You know / by God*
As God me help, I laughė when that I think,
How piteously a-night I made them swink.   *work*

How to control husbands: with relentless nagging

But by my fay, I told of it no store: *faith , I didn't care*
They had me given their land and their treasúre,
205 Me needed not do longer diligence[1]
To win their love, or do them reverence.   *respect*
They lovėd me so well, by God above,
That I ne told no dainty of their love.   *I didn't value*
A wisė woman will busy her ever in one   *e. in one = always*
210 To get her love, yea, where as she has none,
But since I had them wholly in my hand,
And since that they had given me all their land,
What should I taken keep them for to please   *take care*
But it were for my profit, or mine ease?   *Unless it were*
215 I set them so a-workė, by my fay,   *faith*
That many a night they sungen 'Welaway!'   *'Alas'*
The bacon was not fetched for them, I trow,   *I guess*
That some men have in Essex at Dunmow.[2]
I governed them so well after my law,   *according to*
220 That each of them full blissful was and faw   *glad*
To bringė me gay thingės from the fair.   *pretty*
They were full glad when I spoke to them fair,   *nicely*
For God it wot, I chid them spitously.   *G. knows I nagged t. mercilessly*
    Now hearken how I bore me properly.   *behaved / usually?*
225 You wisė wivės that can understand,
Thus shall you speak and bear them wrong on hand,   *deceive them*
For half so boldėly can there no man
Swear and lie as a woman can.
(I say not this by wivės that be wise,
230 But if it be when they them misadvise).   *unless they misbehave*

---

[1] 205: "I no longer needed to take pains" (lit. "It was no longer necessary to me").

[2] 218: The Dunmow Flitch of bacon, awarded every year to the couple who had not quarreled all year or regretted their marriage.

A wisė wife, if that she can her good,   *if she knows*
Shall bearen him on hand the chough is wood,[1]
And takė witness of her ownė maid
Of her assent. But harken how I said:
235 'Sir oldė kaynard, is this thine array?[2]   *You old fool*
Why is my neighėbourė's wife so gay?   *so well dressed*
She is honourėd overall there she goes.   *everywhere*
I sit at home; I have no thrifty clothes.   *pretty*
What dost thou at my neigėhbourė's house?
240 Is she so fair? Art thou so amorous?
What rown you with our maid, ben'dicitee?   *whisper / bless us!*
Sir oldė lecher, let thy japės be.   *games*
And if I have a gossip or a friend   *a confidant*
Withouten guilt, thou chidest as a fiend   *you complain like a devil*
245 If that I walk or play unto his house.   *enjoy myself at*
Thou comest home as drunken as a mouse
And preachest on thy bench — with evil preef!   *evil take you!*

What husbands preach and complain about — marriage, mostly

Thou sayst to me it is a great mischief
To wed a poorė woman for costáge.   *expense*
250 And if that she be rich, of high paráge,   *birth*
Then sayst thou that it is a tormentry
To suffer her pride and her meláncholy.
And if that she be fair (Thou very knave!)   *if she's pretty, you wretch*
Thou sayst that every holor will her have;   *lecher*
255 She may no while in chastity abide
That is assailėd upon each a side.[3]   *every side*
Thou sayst some folk desire us for richesse,   *riches*

---

[1] 231-34: " A woman who knows what is good for her will convince her husband that 'the crow is mad', and call her maid to witness for her." In a well-known folktale a talking bird (a chough or crow) sees a woman committing adultery, and tells her husband. But with the help of her maid, the wife is able to convince the husband that the bird is talking nonsense. The wife is less lucky in Chaucer's version of that story, *The Manciple's Tale.*

[2] 235: *thine array* means either "your way of behaving" or (more probably) "the clothes you let me have."

[3] 256: For the 25 lines or so following 256 notice the array of pronouns the Wife uses interchangeably: *us, she, I, their.* She also has a disconcerting habit of switching from *they* to *he* and back when speaking of her husbands.

Some for our shape and some for our fairness,	*beauty*
And some for she can either sing or dance,	
260 And some for gentleness and dalliance,	*playfulness*
Some for their handes and their armes small.	
Thus goes all to the devil, by thy tale.	*account*
Thou sayst men may not keep a castle wall	
It may so long assailed be overall.	*(If) it*
265 And if that she be foul, thou sayst that she	*ugly*
Coveteth every man that she may see,	
For as a spaniel she will on him leap	
Till she may finde some man her to cheap.	*to buy her*
Ne none so gray goose goes there in the lake,	
270 As, sayst thou, that will be without a make,	*mate*
And sayst it is a hard thing for to yield	*give away*
A thing that no man will, his thankes, held.[1]	*gladly take*
Thus sayst thou, lorel, when thou goest to bed,	*old fool*
And that no wise man needeth for to wed,	
275 Nor no man that intendeth unto heaven.	*who hopes to go*
With wilde thunder dint and fiery leven	*thunderbolt & f. lightning*
May thy welked necke be tobroke!	*wrinkled n. be broken*
Thou sayst that dripping houses and eke smoke	*leaky*
And chiding wives maken men to flee	*nagging*
280 Out of their owne house. Ah, ben'citee!	*bless us!*
What aileth such an old man for to chide!	
Thou sayst we wives will our vices hide	
Till we be fast, and then we will them show.	*married*
Well may that be the proverb of a shrew.	*wretch*
285 Thou sayst that oxen, asses, horses, hounds,	
They be assayed at diverse stounds.	*tested at various times*
Basins, lavers, ere that men them buy,	*bowls*
Spoones and stools, and all such husbandry,	*utensils*
And so be pots, clothes, and array;	*& equipment*
290 But folk of wives maken no assay,	*no test*
Till they be wedded. (Olde dotard shrew!)	*senile old fool!*
And then, sayst thou, we will our vices show.	

---

[1] 271-2: A difficult couplet, meaning, perhaps "It is hard to give away a thing that no man will gladly take."

Further charges

	Thou sayst also, that it displeaseth me,	
	But if that thou wilt praisen my beauty,	*Unless*
295	And but thou pore always upon my face,	*look*
	And clepe me fairė dame in every place,	*call / lady*
	And but thou make a feast on thilkė day	*(birthday)*
	That I was born, and make me fresh and gay,	*buy me new clothes*
	And but thou do unto my nurse honoúr,	
300	And to my chamberer within my bower,	*my lady's maid*
	And to my father's folk, and mine allies.	*my relatives*
	Thus sayest thou, old barrel full of lies!	

I accused my husbands of jealousy, possessiveness and cheapness

	And yet of our apprenticė Jankin,	
	For his crisp hair, shining as gold so fine,	
305	And for he squireth me both up and down,	*because he*
	Yet hast thou caught a false suspicïon:	
	I will him not, though thou were dead to-morrow.	*I wouldn't have him*
	But tell me this, why hidest thou— with sorrow!—	*bad luck to you!*
	The keyės of thy chest away from me?	
310	It is *my* good as well as *thine,* pardee.	*my property / by God*
	What, ween'st thou make an idiot of our dame?[1]	
	Now by that lord that callėd is Saint Jame,	
	Thou shalt not bothė — though that thou were wood —	*mad*
	Be master of my body and my good;	
315	That one thou shalt forego maugre thine eyen.	*in spite of y. eyes*
	What helpeth it of me inquire and spyen?	*about me*
	I trow thou wouldest lock me in thy chest.	*I guess*
	Thou shouldest say: 'Fair wife, go where thee lest;	*you please*
	Take your disport; I will not 'lieve no talės;	*Have fun / believe*
320	I know you for a truė wife, Dame Alice.'	
	We love no man, that taketh keep or charge	*takes notice or account*
	Where that we go; we will be at our large.	*we want freedom*
	Of allė men y-blessėd may he be	
	The wise astrologer Daun Ptolemy,	

---

[1] 311: "Do you think (*weenest thou*) that you can make an idiot of this lady?" (herself).

325 That says this proverb in his Almagest:
    'Of allė men his wisdom is the highest,
    That recketh not who has the world in hand.'   *cares not who rules*
    By this provérb thou shalt well understand:
    Have thou enough, what thar thee reck or care   *What need you?*
330 How merrily that other folkės fare?[1]
    For certės, oldė dotard, by your leave,   *certainly, old fool*
    You shall have quaintė right enough at eve.   *sex / evening*
    He is too great a niggard that will wern   *miser / refuse*
    A man to light a candle at his lantern;[2]
335 He shall have never the lessė light, pardee.   *by God*
    Have thou enough, thee thar not 'plainė thee.   *need not complain*

I attacked complaints about expensive clothes, and I claimed my freedom

    Thou sayst also, if that we make us gay   *attractive*
    With clothing and with precïous array,   *ornaments*
    That it is peril of our chastity.
340 And yet—With sorrow!—thou must enforcė thee[3]
    And sayst these words in the apostle's name:
    'In habit made with chastity and shame   *clothing / modesty*
    You women shall apparel you,' quod he,
    'And not in tressėd hair, and gay perree,   *jewelry*
345 As pearls, nor with gold, nor clothės rich.'
    After thy text, nor after thy rubric   *By your book / rule*
    I will not work as muchel as a gnat.
    Thou saidest this, that I was like a cat;
    For whoso that would singe a cat's skin,   *If anyone*
350 Then would the cat well dwellen in its inn;   *home*
    And if the cat's skin be sleek and gay,
    She will not dwell in housė half a day,
    But forth she will ere any day be dawed,   *dawned*
    To show her skin and go a caterwawed.   *caterwauling*

---

[1] 329-30: "If you have enough, why do you care how well other people do?"

[2] 333-4: "He is too great a miser who will refuse a man a light from his lantern." This is the Wife's interesting metaphor for sexual freedom. The word *quaint* is a vulgarism or a euphemism for the female sexual organ. See also later *quoniam* and *belle chose* (literally "beautiful thing").

[3] 340: "And yet, blast you, you have to reinforce your opinion" (by quoting the Bible).

355   This is to say, if I be gay, sir shrew,   *well dressed*
       I will run out, my borel for to show.   *clothing*
       Sir oldė fool, what helpeth thee to spy?
       Though thou pray Argus with his hundred eyes
       To be my wardėcorps, as he can best,   *bodyguard*
360   In faith he shall not keep me but me lest;   *unless I want*
       Yet could I make his beard, so may I thee.[1]

I nagged him about his (imaginary) nagging

       Thou saidest eke, that there be thingės three,   *said also*
       The which things greatly trouble all this earth,
       And that no wightė may endure the fourth.   *no person*
365   O leve sir shrewė, Jesus short thy life!   *O dear / shorten*
       Yet preachest thou and sayst a hateful wife
       Y-reckoned is for one of these mischances.   *Is counted*
       Be there no other manner résemblánces[2]   *Are there no o. kinds?*
       That you may liken your parables to
370   But if a silly wife be one of tho' ?   *poor wife / those*
       Thou likenest ekė woman's love to hell,
       To barren land, where water may not dwell.
       Thou likenest it also to wildė fire;
       The more it burns, the more it has desire
375   To cónsume everything that burnt will be.
       Thou sayest: 'Right as wormės shend a tree,   *destroy*
       Right so a wife destroyeth her husband;
       This knowen they that be to wivės bound.'

An admission

       Lordings, right thus, as you have understand,
380   Bore I stiffly mine old husbands on hand   *boldly deceived*
       That thus they saiden in their drunkenness;
       And all was false, but as I took witness
       On Jankin and upon my niece also.[3]

---

[1] 361: "Still I could deceive him, I promise you." If *thee* is the verb "to prosper" rather than a pronoun, *so may I thee* means "So may I prosper."

[2] 368: Are there no other kinds of comparison?

[3] 382-3: "I called Jankin and my niece as witnesses, although it was all a lie", i.e. her accusations were a fabrication; she was putting words into the mouths of her husbands which they had never spoken.

O Lord, the pain I did them and the woe
385 Full guiltéless, by Godé's sweeté pine!   *suffering*
For as a horse, I couldé bite and whine;
I couldé 'plain and I was in the guilt,   *complain even when*
Or elsé often time I had been spilt.   *ruined*
Whoso that first to millé comes, first grint.   *The one / grinds*
390 I 'plainéd first, so was our war y-stint.[1]   *over*
They were full glad to excusen them full blive[2]   *quickly*
Of things of which they never a-guilt their lives. *never guilty in their lives*
Of wenches would I bearen them on hand,   *accuse falsely*
When that for sick they might unnethé stand,   *sickness / barely*
395 Yet tickled I his hearté for that he
Wend that I had of him so great charity.[3]   *thought / love*

I had a trick for getting out of the house: a false but flattering accusation

I swore that all my walking out by night
Was for to spy on wenches that he dight.   *girls he slept with*
Under that color had I many a mirth.
400 For all such wit is given us in our birth:
Deceit, weeping, spinning, God has give
To women kindly, while that they may live.   *by nature*
And thus of one thing I avaunté me,   *I boast*
At th'end I had the better in each degree,   *in every way*
405 By sleight or force or by some manner thing,   *By trickery*
As by continual murmur or grouching;   *grumbling*

Sexual refusal as a weapon

Namely a-bed, there hadden they mischance,   *Especially / bad luck*
There would I chide, and do them no pleasance.
I would no longer in the bed abide,

---

[1] 389-90: "The first one to the mill is the first to get the corn ground. I complained first, and so the battle was over." Whoever strikes first, wins.

[2] 391-4: "They were glad to be excused quickly from things they had never been guilty of in their lives. I would accuse them of having girls (*wenches*) when they were so sick they could barely stand."

[3] 395-6: "I tickled his vanity by making him think I loved him so." Note again the slippage of pronouns from *they, them* to *his, him* in the preceding lines and below. The same thing happens with *I, us, women* in the following lines, a feature of the Wife's style.

410   If that I felt his arm over my side,
       Till he had made his ransom unto me;
       Then would I suffer him to do his nicety.   *allow him*
       And therefore every man this tale I tell:
       Win whoso may, for all is for to sell.   *whoever can*
415   With empty hand men may no hawkės lure.
       For winning would I all his lust endure,
       And makė me a feignėd appetite,   *desire*
       And yet in bacon had I never delight.   *cured (old) meat*
       That madė me that ever I would them chide.

Relentless nagging

420   For though the Pope had sitten them beside,
       I would not spare them at their ownė board.   *table*
       For by my truth I quit them word for word.
       As help me very God omnipotent,
       Though I right now should make my testament,   *my will*
425   I owe them not a word that it n'is quit.   *isn't repaid*
       I brought it so aboutė by my wit
       That they must give it up, as for the best,
       Or elsė had we never been in rest.
       For though he lookėd as a wood lion,   *angry*
430   Yet should he fail of his conclusïon.

Another tactic: I would ask him to be reasonable and yield

       Then would I say: 'Now, goodė leve, take keep,   *my dear, look*
       How meekly looketh Willikins our sheep!   *W = husband*
       Come near, my spouse, and let me ba thy cheek.   *kiss*
       You should be allė patïent and meek,
435   And have a sweetė spicėd conscïence.   *easy, forgiving*
       Since you so preach of Job's patïence,
       Suffereth always, since you so well can preach,   *Put up with things*
       And but you do, certain we shall you teach   *unless you do*
       That it is fair to have a wife in peace.   *is good*
440   One of us two must bowė doubtėless,
       And since a man is morė reasonable
       Than woman is, you mustė be sufferable.   *tolerant, forbearing*
       What aileth you to grouchė thus and groan?   *grumble*

Is it for you would have my quaint alone?[1]   *my body for yourself*
445 Why, take it all. Lo, have it every deal.   *every bit*
Peter, I shrew you, but you love it well.[2]   *By St. Peter*
For if I wouldė sell my belle chose,   *my body*
I couldė walk as fresh as is a rose,
But I will keep it for your ownė tooth.   *just for you*
450 You be to blame, by God, I say you sooth.'   *truth*
Such manner wordės haddė we in hand.   *together*

My fourth husband played the field, but I got even

Now will I speaken of my fourth husband.
My fourthė husband was a reveller;
This is to say, he had a paramour,   *lover*
455 And I was young and full of ragery,   *passion*
Stubborn and strong, and jolly as a pie.   *magpie*
How I could dancė to a harpė small!
And sing, y-wis, as any nightingale   *indeed*
When I had drunk a draught of sweetė wine.
460 Metellius, the foulė churl, the swine,
That with a staff bereft his wife her life   *robbed*
For she drank wine, though I had been his wife,   *Because / if I*
Ne should he not have daunted me from drink.   *scared*
And after wine, of Venus most I think,
465 For all so siker as cold engenders hail,   *surely / produces*
A likerous mouth must have a likerous tail.[3]
In woman vinolent is no defense,   *full of wine*
This knowen lechers by experience.

A parenthesis: the pleasure of nostalgia — and the regret

But, Lord Christ, when that it remembereth me   *when I remember*
470 Upon my youth, and on my jollity,
It tickleth me about my heartė's root.

---

[1] 444: "Is it because you want my body sexually for yourself alone?" See earlier note on *quaint*. (333-4)

[2] 446: "By St. Peter, I declare that you really love it very much."

[3] 466: Probably a pun on *liquorous* (liquored) and *likerous* (lecherous), as well as on *tail*.

Unto this day it does my heartė boot   *good*
That I have had my world as in my time.
But age, alas! that all will envenime,   *envenom, poison*
475 Hath me bereft my beauty and my pith.   *robbed me / vigor*
Let go! Farewell! The devil go therewith!
The flour is gone; there is no more to tell.
The bran, as I best can, now must I sell.
But yet to be right merry will I fond.   *try*
480 Now will I tellen of my fourth husband.

My revenge

I say I had in heartė great despite,   *jealousy*
That he of any other had delight;   *other (woman)*
But he was quit, by God and by Saint Joce: *repaid*
I made him of the samė wood a cross,
485 Not of my body in no foul mannér,
But certainly I madė folk such cheer,[1]
That in his ownė grease I made him fry
For anger and for very jealousy.
By God, in earth I was his purgatory,
490 For which I hope his soulė be in glory.
For, God it wot, he sat full oft and sung,   *God knows*
When that his shoe full bitterly him wrung.[2]
There was no wight, save God and he, that wist   *that knew*
In many wise how sorely I him twist.   *ways / tortured*
495   He died when I came from Jerusalem,
And lies y-grave under the roodė-beam,   *buried u. t. church cross*
All is his tombė not so curious   *Although / so elaborate*
As was the sepulchre of him, Darius,   *tomb*
Which that Apelles wroughtė subtlely.   *made*
500 It is but waste to bury them preciously.   *expensively*
Let him farewell, God give his soulė rest.
He is now in his grave and in his chest.   *coffin*

---

[1] 486: "I was so pleasant to folk (men) ....," that is, she was a great flirt.

[2] 492: "...when his shoe pinched him severely." He often had to put on a good face when in fact he was hurting badly.

I married my fifth husband for love. **He** managed **me.**

Now of my fifthe husband will I tell.
God let his soule never come in Hell.
505   And yet was he to me the moste shrew;   *roughest*
That feel I on my ribbes all by row,
And ever shall, unto mine ending day.
But in our bed he was so fresh and gay,
And therewithal he could so well me glose,   *sweet-talk me*
510   When that he woulde have my belle chose,   *body*
That, though he had me beat in every bone,
He coulde win again my love anon.   *promptly*
I trow I loved him beste for that he   *I guess / because he*
Was of his love daungerous to me.   *sparing, cool*

515   We women have, if that I shall not lie,
In this matter a quainte fantasy.   *odd caprice*
Wait what thing we may not lightly have,   *Watch whatever*
Thereafter will we cry all day and crave.   *For that*
Forbid us thing, and that desiren we;
520   Press on us fast, and thenne will we flee.
With daunger outen we all our chaffare;[1]   *bring out our goods*
Great press at market maketh dearer ware,   *great demand / goods*
And too great cheap is held at little price.   *market supply*
This knoweth every woman that is wise.

525   My fifthe husband, God his soule bless,
Which that I took for love and not richesse,
He sometime was a clerk of Oxenford,   *was once a student*
And had left school, and went at home to board   *to lodge*
With my gossip, dwelling in our town.   *my confidant*
530   God have her soul, her name was Alison.
She knew my heart and all my privity,   *secrets*
Bet than our parish priest, so may I thee.   *Better / thrive*
To her bewrayed I my counsel all;   *confided*

---

[1] 521-523: "When there is reluctance (*daunger*) to buy, then we bring out all our merchandise (*chaffare*). Great market demand makes things more expensive (*dearer*); too great a supply (*cheap*) reduces the price." If her wares are much in demand, then the customer has to pay heavily; if the customer shows small interest, she has to seduce him to buy.

For, had my husband pissèd on a wall,
535 Or done a thing that should have cost his life,
To her and to another worthy wife
And to my niece which that I lovèd well,   *whom*
I would have told his counsel every deal,
And so I did full often, God it wot,   *God knows*
540 That made his facè often red and hot
For very shame, and blamed himself for he
Had told to me so great a privity.   *secret*

How I wooed Jankin, who became my fifth husband

And so befell that oncè in a Lent,
(So often times I to my gossip went,   *my confidant*
545 For ever yet I lovèd to be gay,   *well dressed*
And for to walk in March, April, and May
From house to house, to hearen sundry talès)
That Jankin Clerk, and my gossip, Dame Alice,
And I myself, into the fieldès went.
550 My husband was at London all that Lent;
I had the better leisure for to play,
And for to see, and eke for to be seen   *also*
Of lusty folk. What wist I where my grace   *lively / did I know / fortune*
Was shapen for to be, or in what place?[1]
555 Therefore made I my visitatìons
To vigils, and to processìons,   *To evening services*
To preachings eke, and to these pilgrimáges,
To plays of miracles,[2] and to marriáges,
And weared upon my gayè scarlet gites.   *And wore / gowns*
560 These wormès nor these mothès nor these mites
(Upon my peril!) fret them never a deal.   *I assure you / ate*
And wost thou why? For they were usèd well.   *know you why?*
      Now will I tellen forth what happened me:
I say, that in the fieldès walkèd we,
565 Till truly we had such dalliance   *playful talk*
This clerk and I, that of my purveyance   *foresight*
I spoke to him, and said him how that he,

---

[1] 553-4: "How could I know what or where my fortune was destined to be?"

[2] 558: Miracle plays (also known as mystery plays) were short plays based on biblical events. Noah's wife in one of these was a forceful character rather like Alison.

If I were widow, shouldė wedden me.
For certainly, I say for no bobbance,   *boasting*
570 Yet was I never without purveyance   *provision*
Of marriage, nor of other thingės eke.   *also*
I hold a mouse's heart not worth a leek,
That has but one hole for to start into,   *run to*
And if that failė, then is all y-do.   *finished*
575 I borė him on hand he had enchanted me   *convinced him*
(My damė taughtė me that subtlety);   *My mother*
And eke I said, I mett of him all night,   *I dreamed*
He would have slain me, as I lay upright,[1]   *face up*
And all my bed was full of very blood;
580 'But yet I hope that you shall do me good,
For blood betokens gold, as me was taught.'
And all was false, I dreamed of it right naught,
But I followėd aye my damė's lore,[2]
As well of that as of other thingės more.
585   But now, sir, let me see, what shall I sayn?
Aha! by God, I have my tale again.

At the funeral of my fourth husband my thoughts were not on the dead

When that my fourthė husband was on bier,
I wept algate and madė sorry cheer,[3]   *indeed / acted sad*
As wivės mustė, for it is uságe,   *custom*
590 And with my kerchief covered my viságe;   *face*
But, for that I was purveyed of a make,[4]   *provided w. a mate*
I wept but small, and that I undertake.   *I promise you*
To churchė was my husband borne a-morrow   *in morning*
With neighėbours that for him madė sorrow,
595 And Jankin, ourė clerk, was one of tho'.   *those*
As help me God, when that I saw him go
After the bier, methought he had a pair
Of leggės and of feet so clean and fair
That all my heart I gave unto his hold.

---

[1] 577-79: The sexual implication of her pretend dreamwork is fairly obvious.

[2] 583: "I followed always my mother's teaching."

[3] 588: "I wept indeed, and put on a sad appearance."

[4] 591: "Because I was assured of (or provided with) a husband."

600 He was, I trowė, twenty winters old	*I guess, 20 years*
And I was forty, if I shall say sooth,	*truth*
But yet I had always a coltė's tooth.	*youthful taste*

My attractions

Gat-toothed I was, and that became me well:	*gap-toothed*
I had the print of Saintė Venus' seal.[1]	
605 As help me God, I was a lusty one,	
And fair, and rich, and young, and well begone;	*well endowed*
And truly, as mine husbands toldė me,	
I had the bestė quoniam might be,	*"chamber of Venus"*
For certės I am all Venerian	
610 In feeling, and my heart is Martian;	
Venus me gave my lust and likerousness,	*sexual desire*
And Mars gave me my sturdy hardiness.	
Mine áscendent was Taur, and Mars therein.	*sign was Taurus*

I loved sex

Alas! alas! that ever love was sin!	
615 I followed aye mine inclinatïon	*always*
By virtue of my constellatïon[2]	
That madė me that I could not withdraw	
My chamber of Venus from a good fellow.	*My quoniam*
Yet have I Mars's mark upon my face,	
620 And also in another privy place.	*private*
For God so wise be my salvatïon,	
I lovėd never by no discretïon,	*calculation*
But ever followėd mine appetite	*desire*
All were he short or long or black or white.	*Whether he was*
625 I took no keep, so that he likėd me,	
How poor he was, nor eke of what degree.[3]	*social rank*

---

   [1] 604: She was gap-toothed, a mark of Venus, the goddess and planet under whose influence she was born. Being gap-toothed was regarded in the Middle Ages as a sign of a strongly-sexed nature, making one a disciple of Venus, the patron saint (!) of Love. *Venerian* (below) is the adjective from Venus as *Martian* is from Mars, the god of war and the lover of Venus. Lines 609-12 and 619-26 are not in Hgw MS.

   [2] 616: "Given to me by the disposition of the stars at my birth."

   [3] 625-6: " So long as he pleased me, I did not care about his poverty or social rank." *...he liked me* almost certainly means "... he pleased me."

*Within a month I married Jankin and gave him control
of my property (alas), but not of my movements*

	What should I say? but at the monthė's end	
	This jolly clerk Jankin, that was so hend,	*charming*
	Has wedded me with great solemnity,	
630	And to him gave I all the land and fee	*money*
	That ever was me given therebefore,	
	But afterward repented me full sore.	
	He wouldė suffer nothing of my list.[1]	*allow / my wishes*
	By God, he smote me once upon the list,	*struck / ear*
635	For that I rent out of his book a leaf,	*Because I tore*
	That of the stroke mine earė waxed all deaf.	*grew*
	Stubborn I was, as is a lioness,	
	And of my tongue a very jangleress,	*chatterer*
	And walk I would as I had done beforn	
640	From house to house, although he had it sworn;	*forbidden*

*He would quote "authorities" against women
gallivanting about. I paid no heed.*

	For which he oftentimės wouldė preach,	
	And me of oldė Roman gestės teach	*stories*
	How he, Simplicius Gallus, left his wife,	*How a man (named)*
	And her forsook for term of all his life,	
645	Not but for open-headed he her saw	*bareheaded*
	Looking out at his door upon a day.[2]	
	Another Roman told he me by name,	
	That, for his wife was at a summer game	*because*
	Without his witting, he forsook her eke.	*knowledge / also*
650	And then would he upon his Bible seek	*he = Jankin*
	That ilkė proverb of Ecclesiast	*Ecclesiasticus 25:25*
	Where he commandeth and forbiddeth fast:	*firmly*
	'Man shall not suffer his wife go roll about.'	*allow / roam*
	Then would he say right thus withouten doubt:	
655	'Whoso that buildeth his house all of sallows,	*willows*
	And pricketh his blind horse over the fallows,	*spurs / fields*

---

[1] 633: "He would allow none of my wishes."

[2] 645-6: "For nothing more than that he saw her one day looking out the door of the house with her head uncovered."

And suffereth his wife go seeken hallows,   *allows / shrines*
Is worthy to be hangèd on the gallows.'
But all for nought, I settè not an haw   *straw*
660 Of his provérbs, nor of his oldè saw;   *old sayings*
Nor I would not of him corrected be.   *by him*
I hate them that my vices tellen me,
And so do more (God wot) of us than I.   *God knows*
This made him wood with me all utterly;   *angry*
665 I wouldè not forbear him in no case.[1]
Now will I say you sooth, by Saint Thomas,   *truth*
Why that I rent out of his book a leaf,   *tore*
For which he smote me, so that I was deaf.   *struck*

His favorite reading was an anti-feminist book

He had a book, that gladly night and day
670 For his desport he would it read alway,   *amusement*
He clepèd it Valere, and Theophrast,[2]
At whichè book he laughed always full fast.
And eke there was sometime a clerk at Rome,   *scholar*
A cardinal that hightè Saint Jerome   *was called*
675 That made a book against Jovinian,
In which book eke there was Tertullian,
Chrysippus, Trotula, and Eloise,
That was abbessè not far from Paris,
And eke the Parables of Solomon,
680 Ovid's Art, and bookès many a one;
And allè these were bound in one volume.[3]
And every night and day was his custom
(When he had leisure and vacation
From other worldly occupatïon)

---

[1] 665: "I would not restrain myself for him under any circumstances".

[2] 671: Two anti-feminist tracts: the *Epistola Valerii* of Walter Map, and the *Liber de Nuptiis* of Theophrastus known only from the large quotations from it that St. Jerome used in his argument against Jovinian.

[3] 681: A very odd anthology, with the Proverbs of Solomon and the work of the ascetic Jerome and Tertullian side by side with Ovid's pagan and sensual "Art of Love," and the sensual, sad but not pagan story of the love of Heloise and Abelard. Presumably the anthologist concentrated on those bits that were derogatory to women, especially married women.

685   To readen in this book of wicked wives.
        He knew of them more legendės and lives
        Than be of goodė wivės in the Bible.
        For trusteth well, it is an impossible,
        That any clerk will speaken good of wives,   *cleric*
690   (But if it be of holy saintės' lives)   *Unless*
        Nor of no other woman never the mo'.

Who writes these books?

        Who painted the lion, tell me, who?[1]
        By God, if women haddė written stories
        As clerkės have within their oratories,   *cloisters*
695   They would have writ of men more wickedness
        Than all the mark of Adam may redress.   *race of A, i.e. men*
        The children of Mercury and of Venus
        Be in their working full contrarious.   *opposed*
        Mercury loveth wisdom and sciénce,   *knowledge*
700   And Venus loveth riot and dispense.   *parties & extravagance*
        And for their diverse dispositïon
        Each fails in other's exaltatïon.   *domination*
        As thus, God wot, Mercury is desolate
        In Pisces, where Venus is exaltate,
705   And Venus fails where Mercury is raised.[2]
        Therefore no woman of no clerk is praised;
        The clerk when he is old, and may naught do   *nothing*
        Of Venus' workės worth his oldė shoe,   *sexual activity*
        Then sits he down, and writes in his dotáge,   *senility*
710   That women cannot keep their marrïáge.

From Jankin's Book of Wicked Wives: Biblical examples

        But now to purpose, why I toldė thee,
        That I was beaten for a book, pardee.   *by God*

---

[1] 692: A man and a lion see a representation of a man overpowering a lion. The lion questions the truth and accuracy of this picture: clearly a man and not a lion had produced it, he said; if lions could paint or sculpt, the representation would be totally reversed.

[2] 697-705: The fancy astrological detail makes the simple point that people of such opposite tastes and temperaments do not get on well together and do not present flattering pictures of each other. Professional celibates had a higher opinion of themselves than of married people, let alone of enthusiasts for sensuality like Alison of Bath. For an elaborate discussion of the Wife's horoscope see J.D. North, *Chaucer's Universe*, pp. 289 ff.

Upon a night, Jankin that was our sire,   *man of house*
Read in his book, as he sat by the fire,
715   Of Eva first, that for her wickedness   *because of*
Was all mankindė brought to wretchedness,[1]
For which that Jesus Christ himself was slain,
That bought us with his heartė's blood again.   *redeemed us*
Lo here, express of woman may you find,
720   That woman was the loss of all mankind.
Then read he me how Samson lost his hairs:[2]   *Judges XVI, 15-20*
Sleeping, his lemman cut them with her shears,   *lover*
Through whichė treason lost he both his eyen.

Classical examples

Then read he me, if that I shall not lien,
725   Of Hercules, and of his Dianire,
That causėd him to set himself a-fire.[3]
Nothing forgot he the sorrow and the woe,
That Socrates had with his wivės two;
How Xantippė cast piss upon his head.[4]
730   This silly man sat still, as he were dead.   *poor man*
He wiped his head; no morė durst he sayn,   *dared he say*
But: 'Ere that thunder stints there comes a rain.'   *Before the t. stops*
Of Pasiphae, that was the queen of Crete,

---

[1] 715 -20: Eve, the first woman, ate the fruit of the Forbidden Tree in the Garden of Eden. In turn, she induced her husband Adam to eat of the fruit against God's commandment, and as a result they and all their descendants were excluded from Paradise. This human sin against God could only be atoned for by a God-man; hence the human race had to be redeemed by the death of Jesus Christ who was God become man.

[2] 721-3: Samson, a man of immense God-given strength, was seduced by his faithless lover, Dalilah, to tell her the secret of his strength which lay in his hair. While he was sleeping, the Philistines cut off his hair, blinded and enslaved him. He serves as another Biblical example of a strong man brought low by the wiles of a woman.

[3] 726: Dianira, the wife of Hercules, gave him the poisoned shirt of Nessus thinking that it had magical properties which would renew his affections for her. It poisoned him instead, and he burned himself with hot coals.

[4] 728-32: A version of a story told by St Jerome in his anti-marriage argument in the tract Against Jovinian: Socrates laughed at his two wives quarreling over a man as ugly as he was. Then one of them turned on him with the result mentioned. Socrates is an example of even a wise man's unhappy experience with women.

For shrewedness him thought the talė sweet.[1]   *nastiness*
735   Fie, speak no more! It is a grisly thing
      Of her horrible lust and her liking.   *(for a bull)*
         Of Clytemnestra for her lechery,
      That falsely made her husband for to die,[2]   *(Agamemnon)*
      He read it with full good devotïon.
740   He told me eke, for what occasïon   *also / cause*
      Amphiorax at Thebės lost his life.
      My husband had a legend of his wife
      Eriphilë, that for an ouche of gold,   *brooch*
      Has privily unto the Greekės told
745   Where that her husband hid him in a place,   *"Thebaid", Bk VII*
      For which he had at Thebės sorry grace.[3]   *bad fortune*
      Of Livia told he me, and of Lucy.
      They bothė made their husbands for to die;
      That one for love, that other was for hate.
750   Livia her husband on an evening late
      Empoisoned has, for that she was his foe.
      Lucia likerous loved her husband so   *jealous*
      That for he should always upon her think,   *(So) that*
      She gave him such a manner lovė-drink
755   That he was dead ere it were by the morrow;
      And thus algatės husbandės have sorrow.   *always*
         Then told he me, how that one Latumius
      Complained unto his fellow Arius,
      That in his garden growėd such a tree
760   On which he said how that his wivės three
      Hangėd themselves for heartės dėspitous.   *out of spite*
      'O levė brother,' quod this Arius,   *dear*
      'Give me a plant of thilkė blessėd tree,   *of that*
      And in my garden planted shall it be.'
765   Of later date of wivės had he read,
      That some had slain their husbands in their bed,

---

[1] 734-36: Pasiphae, wife of Minos of Crete, fell in love with the bull from the sea and hid herself in a cow constructed specially by Daedalus so that she could copulate with the bull. The result was the monster Minotaur.

[2] 737-8: Clytemnestra, with her lover's help, murdered her husband Agamemnon on his return from the Trojan War.

[3] 740-6: Eryphele was bribed to get her husband to join the war against Thebes in which he was killed.

And let their lecher dight them all the night   *cover*
While that the corpse lay on the floor upright.   *face up*
And some have driven nails into their brain
770   While that they slept, and thus they have them slain.
Some have them given poison in their drink.
He spoke more harm than hearté may bethink.

Anti-feminist proverbs

And therewithal he knew of more provérbs,   *moreover*
Than in this world there growen grass or herbs.
775   'Bet is,' quod he, 'thine habitaïon   *It's better*
Be with a lion, or a foul dragon,   *Ecclesiasticus 15: 16*
Than with a woman using for to chide.'   *always scolding*
'Bet is,' quod he, 'high in the roof abide,   *Better*
Than with an angry wife down in the house.   *Prov. 21: 9*
780   They be so wicked and contrarious
They haté what their husbands loven, aye.'   *always*
He said: 'A woman casts her shame away,
When she casts off her smock; and furthermore,   *her shift*
A fair woman, but she be chaste also,   *pretty / unless*
785   Is like a gold ring in a sowé's nose.'   *Proverbs 11:22*

Tired of his anti-feminist readings and quotations, I acted. A battle ensued.

Who coulde weené, or who could suppose   *c. think or estimate*
The woe that in my heart was, and the pine!   *resentment*
And when I saw that he would never fine   *finish*
To readen on this curséd book all night,
790   All suddenly three leavés have I plight   *plucked*
Out of his book, right as he read, and eke   *and also*
I with my fist so took him on the cheek   *punched*
That in our fire he fell backward adown.
And up he starts as does a wood lion,   *jumped / angry*
795   And with his fist he smote me on the head
That on the floor I lay as I were dead.   *so that*
And when he saw how stillé that I lay,
He was aghast, and would have fled his way,
Till at the last out of my swoon I braid: *I woke*
800   'Oh, hast thou slain me, falsé thief ?' I said,
'And for my land thus hast thou murdered me?

Ere I be dead, yet will I kissen thee.'   *Before I die*
And near he came, and kneelėd fair adown,
And saidė: 'Dearė sister Alison,
805 As help me God I shall thee never smite;   *strike*
What I have done it is thyself to wite,   *blame*
Forgive it me, and that I thee beseech.'
And yet eftsoons I hit him on the cheek,   *promptly*
And saidė: 'Thief! thus much am I wreak.   *avenged*
810 Now will I die, I may no longer speak.'

My husband's surrender and our reconciliation

But at the last, with muchė care and woe
We fell accorded by ourselvės two.   *were reconciled*
He gave me all the bridle in my hand
To have the governance of house and land,
815 And of his tongue, and of his hand also,
And made him burn his book anon right tho.   *promptly right there*
And when that I had gotten unto me
By mastery all the sovereignty,   *control*
And that he said: 'Mine ownė truė wife,
820 Do as thee list the term of all thy life,   *as you please, the length*
Keep thine honoúr, and keep eke mine estate' —[1]
After that day we never had debate.   *argument*
God help me so, I was to him as kind
As any wife from Denmark unto Inde,   *India*
825 And also true, and so was he to me.
I pray to God that sits in majesty
So bless his soulė, for His mercy dear.
Now will I say my tale, if you will hear.

Interruption: A Quarrel between the Summoner and the Friar

The Friar laughed when he had heard all this.
830 "Now, Dame," quod he, "so have I joy or bliss,[2]
This is a long preamble of a tale."   *preface to*

---

[1] 821: This line seems to mean something like "Keep your liberty and also control of my property" but that stretches the meaning of *honour*. It might mean: "Guard your chastity (or good name) and respect my position as your husband."

[2] 830: "Now, Ma'am, as sure as I hope to be saved ..." As in line 164 above, "Dame" is polite usage, not slang.

And when the Summoner heard the Friar gale,   *spout*
"Lo," quod this Summoner, "Godė's armės two!
A friar will intermit him evermore.   *interpose himself always*
835   Lo, goodė men, a fly and eke a frere   *& also a friar*
Will fall in every dish and eke mattér.
What speak'st thou of preámbulatïon?
What! Amble or trot or peace or go sit down.   *be quiet*
Thou lettest our disport in this mannér."   *You spoil our fun*
840   "Yea, wilt thou so, Sir Summoner?" quod the Frere.
"Now by my faith I shall, ere that I go,
Tell of a Summoner such a tale or two,
That all the folk shall laughen in this place."
"Now elsė, Friar, I will beshrew thy face,"   *damn*
845   Quod this Summoner, "and I beshrewė me,   *I'll be damned*
But if I tellė talės two or three   *If I do not*
Of friars, ere I come to Sittingbourne,
That I shall make thy heartė for to mourn;
For well I wot thy patïence is gone."   *I know*
850   Our hostė crïed: "Peace, and that anon,"   *at once*
And saidė: "Let the woman tell her tale.
You fare as folk that drunken be of ale.
Do, Dame, tell forth your tale, and that is best."   *Go on, ma'am*
"All ready, sir," quod she, "right as you lest,   *please*
855   If I have licence of this worthy Frere."   *permission*
"Yes, Dame," quod he, "tell forth, and I will hear."[1]

---

[1] 856: The outbreak of hostilities between two pilgrims sets up two further tales which will fulfill these threats: the Friar later tells a rather good tale involving the iniquity of summoners. The Summoner, in turn, retorts with a rather rambling tale about a greedy friar.

THE WIFE OF BATH'S TALE

Fairies in King Arthur's Britain

In the olden days of King Arthúr,
Of which that Britons speaken great honoúr,
All was this land fulfillèd of faérie;
860 The Elf-Queen, with her jolly company,
Dancèd full oft in many a greenè mead.   *meadow*
This was the old opinion as I read.
I speak of many hundred years ago,
But now can no man see no elvès mo',   *anymore*
865 For now the greatè charity and prayers
Of limiters and other holy freres,[1]
That searchen every land and every stream,
As thick as motès in the sunnè-beam,
Blessing hallès, chambers, kitchens, bowers,   *bedrooms*
870 Cities, boroughs, castles, highè towers,
Thorps and barns, shippens and dairiès—   *Villages / sheep pens*
This maketh that there be no fairiès,
For there as wont to walken was an elf,   *used to*
There walketh now the limiter himself   *begging friar*
875 In undermelès and in mornings,   *early and later a.m.*
And says his matins and his holy things   *morning prayers*
As he goes in his limitation.   *rounds*
Women may go now safely up and down.
In every bush and under every tree,
880 There is no other incubus but he,   *impregnating spirit*
And he ne will not do them but dishonour.[2]

---

[1] 866: *limiters* were mendicant friars (*freres*) licensed to beg within a given limited district.

[2] 881. A difficult line. It appears to mean "He will only dishonor them." Commentators get some sense out of that by pointing out that the "real" incubus, a night spirit who "came upon" women, not only "dishonored" them but impregnated them so that they bore little devils. MS Cam reads "he will do him(self) no dishonour" which makes sense in a different way, but lacks the bite of the preceding lines.

Crime and punishment

And so befell it, that this king Arthúr
Had in his house a lusty bachelor,   *young knight*
That on a day came riding from the river
885 And happened, that, alone as she was born,
He saw a maiden walking him beforn,
Of whichė maid anon, maugre her head,   *against her will*
By very force he raft her maidenhead,   *robbed her virginity*
For which oppressïon was such clamoúr
890 And such pursuit unto the king Arthúr
That damnėd was this knight for to be dead   *condemned*
By course of law, and should have lost his head,
(Peráventure such was the statute tho),   *It seems / then*
But that the queen and other ladies mo'   *more*
895 So longė prayėden the king of grace   *for mercy*
Till he his life him granted in the place,
And gave him to the queen, all at her will,
To choose whether she will him save or spill.   *destroy*

The Queen will pardon the offender on one condition

The queen thankėd the king with all her might;
900 And after this thus spoke she to the knight
When that she saw her time upon a day:
'Thou standest yet,' quod she, 'in such array,   *position*
That of thy life yet hast thou no surety;
I grant thee life, if thou canst tellen me,
905 What thing is it that women most desiren.
Beware, and keep thy neckė-bone from iron.
And if thou canst not tell it me anon,   *at once*
Yet will I give thee leavė for to gon   *to go*
A twelvemonth and a day, to seek and lere   *learn*
910 An answer suffisant in this mattér.   *satisfactory*
And surety will I have, ere that thou pace,   *assurance / go*
Thy body for to yielden in this place.'   *surrender*
Woe was the knight, and sorrowfully he sigheth.
But what? he may not do all as him liketh.   *as he pleases*
915 And at the last he chose him for to wend   *go away*
And come again right at the yearė's end
With such answer as God would him purvey,   *provide*
And takes his leave and wendeth forth his way.

He seeketh every house and every place,
920   Where as he hopeth for to finden grace,   *good fortune*
To learn what thingė women loven most.

He gets various answers to the Queen's question.
The Wife comments on them

But he ne could arriven in no coast,   *country*
Where as he mightė find in this mattér
Two creatures according in fere.   *agreeing together*
925   Some saidė women loven best richesse,
Some said honoúr, some saidė jolliness,
Some rich array, some saidė lust a-bed,   *expensive clothes*
And often times to be widow and wed.
Some saidė that our heartė is most eased
930   When that we be y-flattered and y-pleased.[1]
He goes full nigh the sooth, I will not lie;   *near the truth*
A man shall win us best with flattery;
And with attendance and with busyness   *great attentiveness*
Be we y-limėd bothė more and less.   *caught, ensnared*
935   And somė sayen that we loven best
For to be free, and do right as us lest,   *as we please*
And that no man reprove us of our vice
But say that we be wise and nothing nice.   *silly*
For truly there is none of us all,
940   If any wight will claw us on the gall,   *person / sore spot*
That we n'ill kick for that he says us sooth.[2]   *won't kick / truth*
Assay, and he shall find it that so doth.   *Try*
For be we never so vicïous within,[3]
We will be holden wise and clean of sin.   *want to be thought*
945   And somė say that great delight have we
For to be holden stable and eke secree,   *discreet with secrets*
And in one purpose steadfastly to dwell,
And not bewrayen things that men us tell.   *disclose*
But that tale is not worth a rakė-stele.   *rake handle*
950   Pardee, we women cannė nothing hele.   *By God / can hold nothing in*
Witness on Midas; will you hear the tale?

---

[1] 930 ff: Note the characteristic slippage from *women* to *we / our* to *I* to *us*.

[2] 939-41: "There isn't one of us who will not strike out at someone who touches our sore spot by telling the truth."

[3] 943: "No matter how vicious we are inside ..."

A classical anecdote to illustrate the point that women cannot keep secrets

	Ovid, amongst other thingès small,	*(the Latin poet)*
	Said Midas haddè under his long hairs	
	Growing upon his head two ass's ears;	
955	For whichè vice he hid, as he best might,	*this defect*
	Full subtlely from every mannè's sight,	*v. cleverly*
	That, save his wife, there wist of it no mo'.	*no one else knew*
	He loved her most, and trusted her also.	
	He prayèd her, that to no creätúre	
960	She should not tellen of his dísfigúre.	*disfigurement*
	She swore him: Nay, for all this world to win,	*to him*
	She would not do that villainy nor sin	*dishonor*
	To make her husband have so foul a name;	
	She would not tell it for her ownè shame.	
965	But natheless her thoughtè that she died	*would die*
	That she so longè should a counsel hide;	*secret*
	Her thought it swelled so sore about her heart	*It seemed to her*
	That needèly some word her must astart;[1]	
	And since she durst not tell it to no man,	*dared*
970	Down to a marshè fastè by she ran.	
	Till she came there, her heartè was afire,	
	And as a bittern bumbleth in the mire,	*bird calls in t. mud*
	She laid her mouth unto the water down.	
	'Bewray me not, thou water, with thy sound,'	*Betray*
975	Quod she, 'To thee I tell it, and no mo',	
	Mine husband has long ass's earès two.	
	Now is mine heart all whole, now it is out.	
	I might no longer keep it, out of doubt.'	*without doubt*
	Here may you see, though we a time abide,	
980	Yet out it must, we can no counsel hide.	
	The remnant of the tale, if you will hear,	
	Read Ovid, and there you may it lere.[2]	*learn*

---

[1] 968: "That of necessity some word would have to escape her."

[2] 982: *Metamorphoses* XI, 174-193, where you would learn that it was his barber and not his wife who knew his secret and whispered it into a hole near the water out of which later grew reeds that continually whispered in the wind: "Midas has ass's ears."

Back to the tale: the knight sets out for home
without a satisfactory answer

This knight, of which my tale is specially,
When that he saw he might not come thereby,   *discover it*
985 (This is to say, what women loven most)
Within his breast full sorrowful was the ghost.   *spirit*
But home he goes, he mighté not sojourn,   *delay*
The day was come that homeward must he turn.
And on his way, it happened him to ride
990 In all this care, under a forest side,   *a forest's edge*
Whereas he saw upon a dancé go   *Where*
Of ladies four-and-twenty and yet mo'.
Toward the whiché dance he drew full yern,   *eagerly*
In hopé that some wisdom he should learn;
995 But certainly, ere he came fully there,
Vanishéd was this dance, he wist not where;   *knew*

He meets an ugly old woman

No creäturé saw he that bore life,
Save on the green he saw sitting a wife —   *older woman*
A fouler wight there may no man devise.   *uglier creature / imagine*
1000 Against this knight this old wife gan arise,   *At the approach of*
And said: 'Sir Knight, here forth ne lies no way.[1]
Tell me what you seeken, by your fay.   *faith*
Peráventure it may the better be;   *Perhaps*
These oldé folk can muchel thing,' quod she.   *know a lot*
1005 'My levé mother,' quod this knight, 'certáin,   *My dear*
I n'am but dead, but if that I can sayn[2]
What thing it is that women most desire.
Could you me wiss, I would well quit your hire.'[3]
'Plight me thy truth here in mine hand,' quod she,   *Give your word*
1010 'The nexté thing that I require of thee
Thou shalt it do if it lie in thy might,

---

[1] 1001: At the approach of this Knight the old woman rose and said: "There is no way through here."

[2] 1006: "I am as good as dead unless I can say."

[3] 1008: "If you could inform me (*me wiss*), I would reward (*quit*) you well for your trouble."

And I will tell it you ere it be night.'
'Have here my truthė,' quod the knight, 'I grant.'
'Then,' quod she, 'I dare me well avaunt   *boast*
1015   Thy life is safe, for I will stand thereby   *I guarantee*
Upon my life the queen will say as I.
Let's see which is the proudest of them all
That weareth on a kerchief or a caul,   *women's headdresses*
That dare say nay of what I shall thee teach.   *contradict*
1020   Let us go forth withouten longer speech.'

The old woman gives him the answer to the Queen's question,
and they go to the royal court together

Then rownėd she a 'pistle in his ear,[1]   *whispered a message*
And bade him to be glad, and have no fear.
  When they be comen to the court, this knight
Said he had held his day as he had hight,   *kept / promised*
1025   And ready was his answer as he said.
Full many a noble wife and many a maid
And many a widow (for that they be wise),
The queen herself sitting as justice,
Assembled be this answer for to hear,
1030   And afterward this knight was bid appear.
To every wight commanded was silence,   *every person*
And that the knight should tell in audience   *in public*
What thing that worldly women loven best.
This knight ne stood not still, as does a beast,
1035   But to this questïon anon answered   *promptly*
With manly voice, that all the court it heard: *so that*
'My liegė lady, generally,' quod he,   *My lady Queen*
'Women desiren to have sovereignty
As well over their husband as their love,
1040   And for to be in mastery him above.
This is your most desire, though you me kill.   *greatest*
Do as you list, I am here at your will.'   *wish*
In all the court ne was there wife nor maid
Nor widow, that contráried what he said,   *contradicted what*
1045   But said that he was worthy have his life.

---

[1] 1021: " 'pistle" is short for "epistle" from L. "epistola" = letter, hence a
message of some kind.

The old woman demands her reward

And with that word up started that old wife
Which that the knight saw sitting on the green.
'Mercy,' quod she, 'my sovereign lady queen,   *Please*
Ere that your court depart, as do me right.   *Before*
1050 I taughtė this answer unto the knight,
For which he plighted me his truthė there,   *pledged his word*
The firstė thing I would of him require,
He would it do, if it lay in his might.
Before the court then pray I thee, Sir Knight,'
1055 Quod she, 'that thou me take unto thy wife,
For well thou wost, that I have kept thy life.   *know / saved*
If I say false, say nay, upon thy fay.'   *on your faith (word)*
This knight answered: 'Alas and welaway!
I wot right well that such was my behest.   *I know / promise*
1060 For Godė's love, as choose a new request.
Take all my goods, and let my body go.'
'Nay, then,' quod she, 'I shrew us bothė two,   *a curse on*
For though that I be foul and old and poor,
I n'ould for all the metal nor the ore,   *I would not*
1065 That under earth is grave, or lies above,   *buried*
But if thy wife I were and eke thy love.'[1]   *unless I were*
'My love?' quod he, 'nay, my damnatïon!
Alas! that any of my natïon   *family*
Should e'er so foulė disparágėd be.'[2]   *degraded*

Unwillingly and ungraciously the knight
keeps his promise to the old woman

1070 But all for nought; the end is this, that he
Constrainėd was; he needės must her wed,
And taketh this old wife, and goes to bed.
Now, woudė some men say peráventure,
That for my negligence I do no cure   *take no care*

---

[1] 1064-66: "I would not (be satisfied) with all the (precious) metal and ore below ground and above unless I became your wife and your beloved." That is, "I want more than anything else to be your wife."

[2] 1069: *Disparaged* literally meant being forced to marry someone below one's rank.

1075	To tellen you the joy and all th'array	*splendor*
	That at the feasté was that ilké day.	*same*
	To which thing shortly answeren I shall:	
	I say there was no joy nor feast at all;	
	There n'as but heaviness and muchel sorrow:	*nothing but*
1080	For privily he wedded her a-morrow;	*privately / in the morning*
	And all day after hid him as an owl,	
	So woe was him, his wifé looked so foul.	*So unhappy / ugly*
	Great was the woe the knight had in his thought	
	When he was with his wife a-bed y-brought;	
1085	He walloweth, and he turneth to and fro.	*tosses*
	This oldé wife lay smiling evermo',	
	And said: 'O dearé husband, ben'citee,	*bless me!*
	Fares every knight thus with his wife as ye?[1]	
	Is this the law of king Arthuré's house?	
1090	Is every knight of his thus daungerous?	*cool, distant*
	I am your owné love, and eke your wife,	*also*
	I am she that savéd hath your life.	
	And certés yet did I you never unright.	*harm*
	Why fare you thus with me this firsté night?	
1095	You faren like a man had lost his wit.	*You act*
	What is my guilt?[2] For God's love tell me it,	
	And it shall be amended, if I may.'	
	'Amended!' quod this knight, 'alas! nay, nay.	
	It will not be amended never mo'.	
1100	Thou art so loathly, and so old also,	*so ugly*
	And thereto comen of so low a kind,	*also / a family*
	That little wonder is though I wallow and wind;	*twist & turn*
	So wouldé God mine hearté wouldé burst.'	
	'Is this,' quod she, 'the cause of your unrest?'	
1105	'Yea, certainly,' quod he, 'no wonder is.'	
	'Now, Sir,' quod she, 'I could amend all this,	
	If that me list, ere it were dayés three,	*If it pleased me*
	So well you mighté bear you unto me.[3]	

---

[1] 1088-90: *Fares ...daungerous:* "Does every knight treat his wife this way? Is this some (peculiar) law in King Arthur's court? Is every knight as cold (as you)?"

[2] 1096: "What have I done wrong?"

[3] 1108: "If you were polite to me" or "So that you would be affectionate to me."

The old wife answers the first objection to her: that she is not "gently" born

But for you speaken of such gentilesse,   *But because*
1110 As is descended out of old richesse,
That therefore shouldė you be gentlemen;[1]
Such arrogancė is not worth a hen.
Look who that is most virtuous alway
Privy and apert, and most intendeth aye[2]   *(In) private & public*
1115 To do the gentle deedės that he can,
Take him for the greatest gentleman.
Christ wills we claim of Him our gentilesse,
Not of our elders for their old richesse.   *ancestors*
For though they gave us all their heritáge,
1120 For which we claim to be of high paráge,   *birth*
Yet may they not bequeathen, for no thing,   *in no way*
To none of us, their virtuous living,
That made them gentlemen y-callėd be,
And bade us follow them in such degree.[3]

Dante and others on heredity and gentilesse

1125 Well can the wisė poet of Florénce
That hightė Dante speak of this senténce.   *named D./ this idea*
Lo, in such manner rhyme is Dante's tale:
'Full seld uprises by his branches small   *seldom*
Prowess of man, for God of his goodness
1130 Wills that of Him we claim our gentilesse";[4]

---

[1] 1111: The words "gentilesse," "gentle," "gentleman," "gentry" recur persistently in the passage that follows. The young knight gives them the aristocratic meaning: "gentle" birth is a matter of "genes." The wife insists on the moral meaning: no one is born "gentle," but must become so by his own efforts and God's grace. Likewise, "villains" and "churls," the opposites of "gentlemen," are not born but made — by their own vices. I have retained the original form "gentilesse" rather than "gentleness" for what I hope is greater clarity of meaning.

[2] 1113-15: "Note who is most virtuous always, privately and publicly (*privy and apert*) and who always tries (*intendeth aye*) to do…"

[3] 1121-4: *Yet may … degree:* " There is no way they can leave to us the virtuous way of life which caused them to be called gentlemen and to urge us to follow in the same path." The triple negative *not, no, none* is perfectly good grammar for Chaucer's day.

[4] 1128-30: *Full… man:* "Man's moral integrity seldom goes into the branches (descendants) from the main stock," i.e. moral quality is not inherited. *Prowess* = Dante's "probity." *Branches small* are the heirs of "gentle" stock. God wants us to ascribe our "gentility" to His grace.

For of our elders may we nothing claim   *ancestors*
But temporal thing, that may man hurt and maim.
Eke every wight wot this as well as I.   *person / knows*
If gentilesse were planted naturally   *by birth*
1135 Unto a certain lineage down the line,
Privy and apert then would they never fine   *cease*
To do of gentilesse the fair office;[1]   *good works*
They mighten do no villainy nor vice.   *could not do*
     Take fire, and bear it in the darkest house
1140 Betwixt this and the Mount of Caucasus,
And let men shut the doorės, and go thence—
Yet will the fire as fairė lie and burn
As twenty thousand men might it behold;   *as if*
Its office natural aye will it hold,[2]   *Its nature*
1145 Up peril of my life, till that it die.   *= On peril = I swear*
     Here may you see well, how that gentry
Is not annexėd to possessïon,
Since folk ne do their operatïon
Always as does the fire, lo, in its kind.   *its nature*
1150 For God it wot, men may well often find   *God knows*
A lord's son do shame and villainy.
And he that will have price of his gentry,   *wants respect for*
For he was born of a gentle house,   *(Just) Because*
And had his elders noble and virtuous,   *ancestors*
1155 And n'ill himselfė do no gentle deeds,   *n'ill = will not*
Nor follow his gentle ancestor, that dead is —
He is not gentle, be he duke or earl,
For villain's sinful deedės make a churl.
Thy gentilessė is but renomee   *only the renown*
1160 Of thine ancestors, for their high bounty,   *fine qualities*
Which is a strangė thing to thy person.   *foreign to*
For gentilessė comes from God alone.[3]
Then comes our very gentilesse of grace;
It was no thing bequeathed us with our place.   *rank*

---

[1] 1134-37: *If… office*: "If *gentilesse* were a result of being born into a certain family,
then both publicly (*apert*) and privately (*privy*) the members of that family (*lineage*)
would never cease (*fine*) from doing the good that belongs to (*the office of*) gentilesse."

[2] 1144: "It will always (*aye*) function according to its nature."

[3] 1162: "Gentilesse" in line 1162 has *her* meaning—moral quality. In 1159 it has *his*
meaning— "gentle" birth.

1165   Thinketh how noble, as says Valerius,   *(Roman historian)*
       Was thilkė Tullius Hostilius
       That out of poverte rose to high noblesse.
       Read Seneca, and readeth eke Boece,[1]   *Boethius also*
       There shall you see express, that no dread is,   *without doubt*
1170   That he is gentle that does gentle deedės.
            And therefore, leve husband, I thus conclude,   *dear husband*
       All were it that mine ancestors were rude,   *Although / "lowborn"*
       Yet may the highė God, and so hope I,
       Grant me grace to liven virtuously.
1175   Then am I gentle when that I begin
       To liven virtuously and waiven sin.   *give up*

                    The virtues of poverty

       And there as you of poverte me repreeve,[2]
       The highė God, in whom that we believe,
       In willful poverte chose to live His life.
1180   And certės every man, maiden, or wife
       May understand that Jesus, heaven's king,
       Ne would not choose a vicïous living.
       Glad poverte is an honest thing certáin.
       This will Senec' and other clerkės sayn.   *Seneca & other writers*
1185   Whoso that holds him paid of his poverte,   *Whoever is happy in*
       I hold him rich, all had he not a shirt.[3]
       He that covets is a poorė wight,   *creature*
       For he would have what is not in his might.
       But he that naught has, nor coveteth to have,
1190   Is rich, although men hold him but a knave.   *servant*
       Very povértė singeth properly.[4]   *True p. / naturally*

---

   [1] 1168: Seneca: pagan Roman philosopher (d. 65 a.d.). Boethius: Roman philosopher (perhaps Christian, d. 525 a.d.) whose *Consolations of Philosophy* was highly regarded in the Middle Ages. Having the fairytale wife cite these "authorities" is decidedly odd. Here and in the following lines I have retained the original form *poverte*, which has two syllables and seems to be able to stress either; its modern form *poverty* inconveniently has three, with stress invariably on the first.

   [2] 1177 ff: "And whereas you reprove me for my poverty, [I answer that] the high God in whom we believe, deliberately chose to live his life in poverty." She is referring, of course, to Jesus Christ.

   [3] 1185-6: "Whoever is contented in his poverty, him I consider rich even if he does not possess a shirt."

   [4] 1191: "True (i.e. contented) poverty sings by its very nature."

Juvenal says of poverte merrily: *Satire X, 21*
'The pooré man when he goes by the way,   *along the road*
Before the thievés he may sing and play.'   *In front of*
1195   Povérte is hateful good; and, as I guess,
A full great bringer out of busyness;   *diligence*
A great amender eke of sapience   *improver / wisdom*
To him that taketh it in patïence.
Povérte's a thing, although it seem alenge,[1]   *unpleasant (?)*
1200   Possessïon that no wight will challenge.
Povérte full often, when a man is low,
Maketh himself and eke his God to know.
Povérte's a spectacle, as thinketh me,[2]   *glass / seems to me*
Through which he may his very friendés see.   *true friends*
1205   And, therefore, Sir, since that I not you grieve,
Of my povérte no moré me repreve.   *reprove*

Her age and ugliness

Now, Sir, of eld, that you repreven me: *old age*
And certés, Sir, though no authority   *written opinion*
Were in no book, you gentles of honoúr
1210   Say that men should an old wight do favoúr   *respect an old person*
And clepe him "father", for your gentilesse;   *call him f. / courtesy*
And authors shall I finden, as I guess.[3]
Now, where you say that I am foul and old,   *ugly*
Then dread you not to be a cuckéwold.   *cuckold*
1215   For filth and eldé, also may I thee,   *age / I assure you*
Be greaté wardens upon chastity.[4]   *guardians of*
But natheless, since I know your delight,   *pleasure*
I shall fulfill your worldly appetite.   *sexual*

---

[1] 1199: "Alenge," an uncommon word in Chaucer, is generally glossed "miserable" or "wearisome," which hardly fits this couplet.

[2] 1203: "Spectacle" refers to eye glasses or a magnifying glass, or less likely, a mirror.

[3] 1208-1212: "Even if no respected authors had said so, you 'gentry' yourselves say that, out of courtesy, one should respect an old man and call him 'Father.' And I am sure I can find authors who say so."

[4] 1215-16: "Ugliness and age, I assure you, are great preservers of chastity." In *also may I thee* (lit. as I hope to prosper), the last word, *thee*, is the verb *to prosper*.

She offers him a choice between two things

Choose now,' quod she, 'one of these thinges tway: *two*
1220 To have me foul and old till that I die,
And be to you a true and humble wife,
And never you displease in all my life;
Or else you will have me young and fair,
And take your áventure of the repair   *chance / visiting*
1225 That shall be to your house because of me,
(Or in some other place it may well be).[1]
Now choose yourselfe whether that you liketh.   *which one pleases you*
This knight aviseth him, and sore sigheth,   *thinks to himself*
But at the last he said in this mannér:

He lets **her** choose

1230 'My lady and my love, and wife so dear,
I put me in your wise governance.
Choose yourself which may be most pleasánce
And most honoúr to you and me also;
I do no force the whether of the two.[2]   *I don't care*
1235 For as you liketh, it sufficeth me.'   *As you please*
'Then have I got of you mastery,' quod she,
'Since I may choose and govern as me lest?'   *as I please*
'Yea, certes, wife,' quod he, 'I hold it best.'
'Kiss me,' quod she, 'we be no longer wroth,   *angry*
1240 For by my truth I will be to you both,
This is to say, yea, bothe fair and good.   *pretty & faithful*
I pray to God that I may starven wood,   *die mad*
But I to you be all so good and true   *Unless*
As ever was wife, since that the world was new;
1245 And but I be to-morrow as fair to seen   *unless*
As any lady, empress or queen,
That is betwixt the East and eke the West,
Do with my life and death right as you lest.   *as you please*
Cast up the curtain, look how that it is.'

---

[1] 1224-26: "And take your chances with the large number of visitors (*repair*) that will come to our house because of me — or perhaps to someplace else." The alternatives that the wife poses to her husband constitute a *demande d'amour*, a favorite game of medieval writers, and of aristocratic medieval women, according to Andreas Capellanus. The Knight and the Franklin also propose *demandes* in their tales.

[2] 1234: "I do not care which of the two."

The happy result

1250   And when the knight saw verily all this,   *truly*
    That she so fair was, and so young thereto,
    For joy he hent her in his armės two: *he seized*
    His heartė bathėd in a bath of bliss,
    A thousand times a-row he gan her kiss;   *in a row*
1255   And she obeyėd him in every thing
    That mightė do him pleasance or liking.
    And thus they live unto their livės end
    In perfect joy.

A prayer of sorts

        And Jesus Christ us send
    Husbands meekė, young, and fresh a-bed,
1260   And grace to overbide them that we wed.   *to outlive*
    And eke I prayė Jesus short their lives   *also / shorten*
    That will not be governėd by their wives.
    And old and angry niggards of dispense,   *tight spenders*
    God send them soon a very pestilence.   *veritable plague*

THE PARDONER, HIS PROLOGUE AND HIS TALE

The Portrait of the Pardoner from the General Prologue

The **Pardoner** is accompanied on the pilgrimage by the disgusting Summoner who is his friend, his singing partner and possibly his lover. The Pardoner professes to give gullible people pardon for their sins in exchange for money, as well as a view of his pretended holy relics which will bring them blessings. He too is physically repellent: he has thin scraggly hair of which, however, he is absurdly vain, and his high voice and beardlessness suggest that he is not a full man but something eunuch-like, again a metaphor for his barren spiritual state.

	With him there rode a gentle PARDONER	*him = Summoner*
670	Of Rouncival, his friend and his compeer	*colleague*
	That straight was comen from the court of Rome.	*had come directly*
	Full loud he sang "Come hither love to me."[1]	
	This Summoner bore to him a stiff burdoun.	*bass melody*
	Was never trump of half so great a sound.	*trumpet*
675	This pardoner had hair as yellow as wax	
	But smooth it hung as does a strike of flax.	*hank*
	By ounces hung his lockės that he had,	*By strands*
	And therewith he his shoulders overspread.	
	But thin it lay, by colpons, one by one,	*clumps*
680	But hood, for jollity, wearėd he none,	
	For it was trussėd up in his wallet:	*bag*
	Him thought he rode all of the newė jet,	*fashion*
	Dishevelled; save his cap he rode all bare.	*hair loose / bareheaded*
	Such glaring eyen had he as a hare.	*eyes*

---

[1] 672. The rhyme between "Rome / to me" may have been forced or comic even in Chaucer's day; it is impossible or ludicrous today. The Pardoner probably has not been anywhere near Rome; claiming so is simply part of his pitch to the gullible. His relationship to the Summoner is not obvious but appears to be sexual in some way.

685	A vernicle had he sewed upon his cap.[1]	*A pilgrim badge*
	His wallet lay before him in his lap	*bag*
	Bretfull of pardons, come from Rome all hot.[2]	*Crammed full*
	A voice he had as small as hath a goat.	*thin*
	No beard had he nor never should he have;	
690	As smooth it was as it were late y-shave.	*recently shaved*
	I trow he were a gelding or a mare.	*guess*

His "relics"

	But of his craft, from Berwick unto Ware	*trade*
	Ne was there such another pardoner,	
	For in his mail he had a pillowber	*bag / pillowcase*
695	Which that he saidė was Our Lady's veil.	*Our Lady's = Virgin Mary's*
	He said he had a gobbet of the sail	*piece*
	That Saintė Peter had when that he went	
	Upon the sea, till Jesus Christ him hent.	*pulled him out*
	He had a cross of latten full of stones	*brass*
700	And in a glass he haddė piggės' bones.	
	But with these "relics", when that he found	
	A poorė parson dwelling upon land,	*in the country*
	Upon one day he got him more money	
	Than that the parson got in monthės tway;	*two*
705	And thus, with feignėd flattery and japes	*tricks*
	He made the parson and the people his apes.	*fools, dupes*

His skill in reading, preaching and extracting money from people

	But truly to tellen at the last,	
	He was in church a noble ecclesiast.	*churchman*
	Well could he read a lesson and a story.	
710	But alderbest he sang an offertory[3]	*best of all*

---

[1] 685: *Vernicle:* a badge with an image of Christ's face as it was believed to have been imprinted on the veil of Veronica when she wiped His face on the way to Calvary. Such badges were frequently sold to pilgrims.

[2] 686-7: He has filled his bag with bits of paper or parchment purporting to be pardons "hot" from Rome like cakes from an oven. Illiterate people are often impressed by any written document.

[3] 710: *offertory:* the point in the Mass when the people made their offerings to the priest, and to the Pardoner when he was there. The prospect of money put him in good voice.

For well he wisté when that song was sung   *knew*
He musté preach and well afile his tongue   *polish his sermon*
To winné silver as he full well could.   *he knew how*
Therefore he sang the merrierly and loud.

THE PARDONER AND HIS TALE
Introduction

The Pardoner is a sinister character, one of the most memorable on the pilgrimage to Canterbury and in the whole of English literature. The portrait of him in the General Prologue shows him as deficient in body and depraved in soul, his physical attributes or lack of them a metaphor for the sterile spirit that inhabits his body or lurks in it like a toad in a cellar. His appearance arouses not so much disgust as dis-ease, a profound uneasiness.

He is a confidence man operating a game that still flourishes — manipulating people's religious gullibility, their shame, greed, superstition, etc. Like many others after him, he uses a real rhetorical gift to "stir the people to devotion" so that they will give their pennies, and "namely unto me," as he says. Interestingly enough he knows that his eloquent preaching may in fact help people to turn away from their sins; that is all right, provided that he profits in the process, and his profits are not in the spiritual realm, but strictly material — money, wool, cheese, wheat, gold rings.

The Pardoner's trade grew out of a legitimate if dubious church practice that was difficult to understand and easy to abuse — the doctrine and practice of indulgences, the abuses of which were still causing trouble in the sixteenth century and which were the direct cause of Luther's challenge to the Catholic Church that led to the Reformation. The doctrine of indulgences was roughly this: Even when you had confessed your sins, expressed your regret and a determination to try to avoid them in the future, there was still something owing, penance of some kind, which could take various forms: fasting, going on a pilgrimage, saying certain prayers, giving money to the poor or to some other good cause like the building of a church. It was in the last-mentioned that a fatal slippage took place. Careless or unscrupulous people implied that if you gave money to a good cause, which they represented, that act in itself bought forgiveness for your sins, even without confession or contrition. This was not, of course, church teaching. But it was an idea widely disseminated and widely believed, because it satisfied at the same time the need for easy forgiveness in some, and the need for easy money in others. The Pardoner gave false assurances of God's pardon; the deluded sinner gave real money in exchange.

The Pardoner's Prologue is an astonishing soliloquy, a public confession, but a confession without a trace of the repentance that would make us or God want to forgive him. It is astonishing partly because some readers have difficulty believing that anyone would expose himself and his tricks so blatantly to a group of pilgrims of varying ranks in society and varying ranges of education. Critics of the older school who felt that all fiction should approximate the standards of realism of the nineteenth-century novel, found a plausible explanation for the Pardoner's indiscreet garrulousness in the fact that he has a drink of "corny ale" before he begins his tale.

But of course one no longer needs such "realistic" explanations. Two or three days glancing at daytime talk shows on television will convince anyone that some people will publicly confess to, even boast about, depravities most of us did not know existed. Before Chaucer's own time the confession of Faux Semblant in one of his favorite poems, *The Romance of the Rose*, provided a precedent for his Pardoner. He has literary successors too: look at Richard III in Shakespeare's play two hundred years later who is not unlike the Pardoner in some ways — physically and morally deformed and given to making confessional soliloquies. Look too at Iago or Shylock.

They all tell us things about themselves that no person in his right mind would do. But they are not persons, only characters in fictions which expect the audience to share the conventions, in this case the Pardoner's dramatic soliloquy. We accept the convention that in a mounted procession of about thirty people on thirty horses everyone can hear every word of every tale told by any other. This is realistically unlikely. Neither do people tell tales in polished verse. Except in fiction.

At the heart of the sermon / tale that the Pardoner tells is an extended "exemplum", a story told to illustrate a point that the preacher is making. Pardoners had a deservedly bad name for their moral depravity and their selling of religion; they were also known for telling lewd tales in church to keep their audiences amused so that they might be more forthcoming with money at offertory time. According to Wycliffe, many popular preachers, including Pardoners, were notorious for the filthiness of their "exempla," more especially objectionable for being told in church. That is why, when the Host calls on the Pardoner for a tale, "the gentles gan to cry: Let him tell us of no ribaldry." Since the "gentles" have listened with enjoyment already to the very ribald tales of the Miller and the Reeve, they must have been expecting something really objectionable from the Pardoner. It is a delicious irony that this ugly but clever man disappoints their expectations so splendidly with a sermon that would have done credit to a devout and eloquent member of the Order of Preachers.

This story was old when Geoffrey Chaucer put it in the mouth of his Pardoner in the fourteenth century. Like Shakespeare after him, Chaucer did not go in for the kind of "originality" which prides itself on creating new tales from scratch: all the good stories have already been told and lie ready to hand to be re-told and retailed by a new author in a new way for a new audience. That is the way Chaucer thought, — and B. Traven who novelized this tale in the early twentieth century as *The Treasure of the Sierra Madre,* and John Houston who filmed it in the movie of the same name. The originality is in the new way of telling an old story that rises above time and place to touch us again.

One of the striking things about this tale of Chaucer's is that the "exemplum" is told almost exclusively in dialogue, which gives an unusually dramatic flavor to a story that we would loosely call "dramatic" anyway because of its power. But still it is not realistic. Elements of almost pure allegory like the young drunks setting out on a quest to kill Death, and their meeting with the mysterious Old Man are mixed with elements we find realistic, like the youngest making arrangements to buy wine and bottles and poison, and the story he tells to the druggist to get the poison. The mixture is a very potent one. We do not need nineteenth century realism to make a powerful tale.

Having made a "confession" of his dirty tricks, and then told a moving moral tale totally at odds with the personality revealed in his "confession," the Pardoner does something so odd that it has puzzled generations of critics. He finishes the "exemplum" about three bad lads and the untimely death that they bring upon themselves by their own behavior. Then he goes back to the sermoning of which it was a part, denouncing the sin of avarice that caused their death, and then turns to the congregation to ask for generous contributions for the pardons he will give out.

This final plea is in line with all that he has told us about his motives in the prologue to his tale. Then suddenly he has three and a half lines that take us by surprise:

> and lo, sirs, thus I preach.
> And Jesus Christ, that is our soulés' leech,   *(physician)*
> So granté you His pardon to receive,
> For that is best. I will you not deceive.

What has happened? Has a ray of God's grace finally penetrated the soul of this hardened cynic? Such things happen. Has he been so moved by his own powerful sermon that finally he gets the point of it? One would like to think so. But as one is smiling at this satisfactory ending he turns on quite suddenly again his salesman's pitch for the relics he has earlier denounced as spurious to this very audience, and offers to give the Host first go — in return for money, of course. This turn questions our momentary conclusion that the Pardoner has finally seen a ray of light. But the uneasy feeling persists that those three and a half lines were not part of a trick. Is the final pitch and the offer to the Host just the Pardoner's joke that the Host misunderstands or responds to in the wrong way? A number of explanations of the ending are possible, none of them totally satisfactory, leaving the Pardoner an enigma like the Old Man of his tale.

The invitation to the Pardoner to tell a story comes after the Physician has told a gory tale about a judge who abused his position to plot with a low fellow (churl) to abduct a beautiful young woman. Her father beheaded her rather than allow her to be raped. The Host vociferously declares his dissatisfaction with this thoroughly depressing tale, and wants to be cheered up.

>   Our HOST began to swear as he were wood: *mad*
>   "Harrow!" quod he, "By nailés and by blood![1]
>   This was a false churl and a false justice.   *low fellow*
> 290   As shameful death as hearté may devise
>   Come to these judges and their advocates.
>   Algate, this silly maid is slain, alas.   *Still, this poor girl*
>   Alas, too dearé boughté she beauty.

---

[1] 288-9: "Help! By (Christ's) nails and blood." The host here gives a demonstration of the careless swearing about which the Pardoner will soon speak so eloquently and hypocritically.

Wherefore I say all day, that men may see   *So I always say*
295 That gifts of Fortune and of Nature
Be cause of death to many a creature.
Her beauty was her death, I dare well sayn.
Alas, so piteously as she was slain.
Of bothë giftës that I speak of now
300 Men have full often more for harm than prow.   *than benefit*
But truly, mine ownë master dear,
This is a piteous talë for to hear.
But natheless, pass over, is no force.   *it doesn't matter*

The Host tries his heavy hand at making jokes about medicine

I pray to God to save thy gentle corse   *corpse i.e.body*
305 And eke thy urinals and thy jordanes,   *also thy u. & chamber pots*
Thine Hippocras and eke thy Galiens[1]
And every boistë full of thy lectuary —   *every box / medicine*
God bless them, and Our Lady, Saintë Mary.
So may I thee, thou art a proper man   *thee = succeed / fine*
310 And like a prelatë, by Saint Ronian.   *church dignitary*
Said I not well? I cannot speak in term,   *in technicalities*
But well I wot, thou dost mine heart to erme   *well I know / to grieve*
That I have almost caught a cardinacle.   *heart attack*
By corpus bonës, but I have triacle,[2]   *unless / medicine*
315 Or else a draught of moist and corny ale,   *fine & tasty*
Or but I hear anon a merry tale,   *Or unless*
My heart is lost for pity of this maid.

The Host turns to the Pardoner for something amusing

Thou bel ami, thou Pardoner," he said,   *good friend*
"Tell us some mirth or japës right anon."   *jokes*
320 "It shall be done," quod he, "by Saint Ronion.
But first," quod he, "here at this alë stake,   *tavern sign*
I will both drink, and eaten of a cake."

---

[1] 306: *Hippocras* and *Galiens* are the Host's words for what he thinks of as medicinal drinks.

[2] 314: "By God's bones, unless I have some medicine *(triacle)*." Harry's confused oath "By corpus bones" seems to be a confusion between the oath "God's bones" and the corpse that he associates with the physician.

And right anon these gentles 'gan to cry:	*gentlefolk*
"Nay, let him tell us of no ribaldry.	*dirty stories*
325 Tell us some moral thing, that we may lere	*learn*
Some wit, and then will we gladly hear."	*wisdom*
"I grant y-wis," quod he, "but I must think	*certainly*
Upon some honest thing while that I drink."[1]	

THE PROLOGUE of the PARDONER'S TALE

The Pardoner gives a boastful account of how he deludes credulous people with false documents, false relics and a fast tongue.

"Lordings," quod he, "in churches when I preach,	*ladies & gentlemen*
330 I painé me to have a haughty speech	*take pains / impressive*
And ring it out as round as goes a bell.	
For I can all by roté that I tell.	*know all by heart*
My theme is always one, and ever was:	
Radix malorum est cupiditas.[2]	

His "credentials"

335 First I pronouncé whencé that I come	
And then my bullés show I all and some.	*papal letters*
Our liegé lordé's seal on my patent — [3]	*on my letter*
That show I first, my body to warrant.	*to guarantee my person*
That no man be so bold, nor priest nor clerk,	*neither...nor*
340 Me to disturb of Christé's holy work.	
And after that then tell I forth my tales.	
Bulls of popés and of cardinals,	
Of patriarchs and bishopés I show,	
And in Latin I speak a wordés few	

---

[1] 328: On the significance of the pardoner's drink, and the objection of the "gentles" see Introduction to this tale.

[2] 334: "The root of (all) evils is greed." From the Epistle of St. Paul to Timothy VI, 10.

[3] 336-8: "Bull" (Latin "bulla"= a seal) is the name commonly given to official letters from popes, but also from others of high rank. "Liege lord" is ambiguous (deliberately?) and might mean that he is claiming the king's protection or the bishop's or the pope's for his person.

345   To saffron with my predicatïon   *To flavor my sermon*
        And for to stir them to devotïon.

Among his "relics" is a bone that has miraculous powers when dipped in a well

        Then show I forth my longë crystal stones   *glasses*
        Y-crammëd full of clothës and of bones.
        "Relics" be they, as weenen they each one.   *they all think*
350   Then have I in latten a shoulder bone   *in brass jar*
        Which that was of a holy Jewë's sheep.[1]
        'Good men, say I, take of my wordës keep: *take notice*
        If that this bone be washed in any well,
        If cow or calf or sheep or oxë swell
355   That any worm has eat or worm y-stung,[2]
        Take water of that well and wash his tongue,
        And it is whole anon. And furthermore,   *healed at once*
        Of pockës and of scabs and every sore
        Shall every sheep be whole that of this well
360   Drinketh a draught. Take keep eke what I tell: *Heed also*
        If that the goodman that the beastës oweth   *the farmer who owns*
        Will, every week ere that the cock him croweth   *before cockcrow*
        Fasting, drinken of this well a draught,
        As thilkë holy Jew our elders taught,   *As that*
365   His beastës and his store shall multiply.
        And sirs, also it healeth jealousy.
        For though a man be fall in jealous rage,
        Let maken with this water his potáge,[3]   *his soup*
        And never shall he more his wife mistrust
370   Though he the sooth of her defaultë wost,   *truth / knows*
        All had she taken priestës two or three.[4]   *Even if*

A marvelous mitten

        Here is a mitten, eke, that you may see.   *a glove also*
        He that his hand will put in this mittén,

---

[1] 351: This Old Testament holy Jew is conveniently nameless.

[2] 354-5: If any animal swells up that has eaten or been stung by a "worm", take water ...

[3] 368: "Let his soup be made with this water ..."

[4] 369-71: "He will never again mistrust his wife even if he *knows* about her infidelity, and even if she has had 2 or 3 priests as sexual partners"— the basic plot of many a fabliau.

He shall have multiplying of his grain
375   When he has sownė, be it wheat or oats —
So that he offer pennies or else groats.   *Provided / or silver*

Serious sinners will not be able to benefit

Good men and women, one thing warn I you:
If any wight be in this churchė now   *person*
That has done sinnė horrible, that he   *so that he*
380   Dare not for shame of it y-shriven be,   *confess it*
Or any woman, be she young or old
That has made her husband a cuckold —   *has deceived her h.*
Such folk shall have no power nor no grace
To offer to my relics in this place.
385   And whoso findeth him out of such blame,
He will come up and offer in God's name,
And I assoil him by the authority   *I'll absolve*
Which that by bull y-granted was to me.'   *by Pope's letter*

His skill and astuteness in preaching against avarice brings him profit, pride and pleasure

By this gaud have I wonnė, year by year   *this trick*
390   A hundred marks since I was pardoner.
I standė like a clerk in my pulpit,   *a cleric*
And when the lewėd people is down y-set   *ignorant congregation*
I preachė so as you have heard before
And tell a hundred falsė japės more.   *amusing lies*
395   Then pain I me to stretchė forth the neck,
And east and west upon the people I beck
As does a dovė sitting on a barn.
My handės and my tonguė go so yern   *so fast*
That it is joy to see my busyness.
400   Of avarice and of such cursedness
Is all my preaching, for to make them free
To give their pence, and namely unto me.   *pennies*
For my intent is not but for to win,
And nothing for correctïon of sin.
405   I reckė never, when that they be buried   *I don't care*
Though that their soulės go a blackė berried.   *picking blackberries*
For certės many a predicatïon   *sermon*

Comes oftentime of evil intentïon
Some for pleasance of folk and flattery — *to please & flatter people*
410 To be advancèd by hypocricy,
And some for vainè glory, and some for hate.

His revenge on any enemy of pardoners

For when I dare no other way debate, — *respond, hit back*
Then will I sting him with my tonguè smart — *sharp(ly)*
In preaching, so that he shall not astart — *escape*
415 To be defamèd falsely, if that he
Hath trespassed to my brethren or to me. — *offended my colleagues*
For though I tellè not his proper name, — *actual*
Men shall well knowen that it is the same
By signès and by other circumstances.
420 Thus quit I folk that do us displeasances. — *I repay*
Thus spit I out my venom under hue — *color*
Of holiness, to seemen holy and true.

How to profit by preaching against greed and by taking offerings even from the poorest

But shortly mine intent I will devise: — *I'll tell*
I preach of nothing but for covetise. — *greed, avarice*
425 Therefore my theme is yet and ever was:
Radix malorum est cupiditas.
Thus can I preach against that samè vice
Which that I use, and that is avarice. — *which I practice*
But though myself be guilty in that sin,
430 Yet can I maken other folk to twin — *to turn away*
From avarice, and sorè to repent,
But that is not my principal intent;
I preachè nothing but for covetise.
Of this matter it ought enough suffice.
435 Then tell I them examples many a one
Of oldè stories longè time agone.
For lewèd people loven talès old. — *ignorant laymen*
Such thingès can they well report and hold. — *retell & remember*
What? Trowè you that whilès I may preach — *Do you think ...*
440 And winnè gold and silver for I teach — *for teaching*
That I will live in poverte wilfully? — *poverty*

Nay, nay, I thought it never truly.
For I will preach and beg in sundry lands.
I will not do no labor with my hands
445   Nor makė baskettės, and live thereby.
Because I will not beggen idlely,
I willė none of the apostles' counterfeit.[1]
I will have money, woolė, cheese and wheat,
All were it given of the poorest page   *Even if given by*
450   Or of the poorest widow in a villáge,
All should her children starvė for famine.   *Even if*
Nay, I will drinkė liquor of the vine
And have a jolly wench in every town.

But he can tell a moral tale

But hearken, lordings, in conclusïon,   *Ladies & gentlemen*
455   Your liking is that I shall tell a tale.
Now have I drunk a draught of corny ale,
By God, I hope I shall you tell a thing
That shall by reason be at your liking,
For though myself be a full vicious man,
460   A moral tale yet I you tellė can
Which I am wont to preachė for to win.[2]
Now hold your peace. My tale I will begin."

---

[1] 446-7: "Because I will ...": "Because I don't intend to beg in vain" or "Because I don't want to be an idle beggar [as distinct from a working preacher?], I want none of the counterfeit of the apostle / apostles. I want money, cheese, etc." "Counterfeit" here would be a noun meaning something unsubstantial and "useless" like a blessing. But *counterfeit* may be a verb meaning "copy, imitate": "I will imitate none of the apostles."

[2] 461: "Which I am accustomed to preach to make money."

THE PARDONER'S TALE

A story about three young men who gamble,
drink, swear and frequent prostitutes

	In Flanders whilom was a company	*once upon a time*
	Of youngë folk that haunteden folly,	*persisted in*
465	As riot, hazard, stewës, and taverns	*gambling / brothels*
	Where, as with harpës, lutës and gitterns	*guitars*
	They dance, and play at dice both day and night,	
	And eat also and drink over their might	*to excess*
	Through which they do the devil sacrifice	
470	Within that devil's temple in cursëd wise	
	By superfluity abominable.	*excess*
	Their oathës be so great and so damnable	
	That it is grisly for to hear them swear.	
	Our blessëd Lordë's body they to-tear;	*tear apart*
475	Them thought that Jewës rent Him not enough.	*tore*
	And each of them at others' sinnë laugh.	
	And right anon then comë tumblesters	*dancing girls*
	Fetis and small, and youngë fruitesters,	*slim / fruit sellers*
	Singers with harpës, bawdës, waferers,	*pimps, wafer sellers*
480	Which be the very devil's officers	*Who are ... agents*
	To kindle and blow the fire of lechery	
	That is annexëd unto gluttony.	

He slips into a sermon against excess in eating or drinking

	The Holy Writ take I to my witness	*Bible*
	That lechery is in wine and drunkenness.	
485	Lo, how that drunken Lot unkindëly	*unnaturally*
	Lay by his daughters two, unwittingly,	
	So drunk he was he n'istë what he wrought.[1]	*didn't know w.h. did*
	Herod (whoso well the stories sought)[2]	

---

[1] 485-7: See Genesis 19, 30-36 for the unedifying story. Lot's daughters got their father drunk so that they could copulate with him incestuously ("unkindly," against "kind" = Nature).

[2] 488: "Whoever has consulted the story" in Matt. 14 or Mark 6, where he would find that Herod Antipas, Tetrarch ("King") of Galilee, during a feast rashly promised the dancer Salome anything she asked for. Instigated by her mother Herodias, who hated John the Baptist for denouncing her adulterous relationship with Herod, Salome asked for the head of the Baptist on a dish. Herod accordingly had John executed.

	When he of wine replete was at his feast,	*full of wine*
490	Right at his ownė table he gave his hest	*order*
	To slay the Baptist John full guiltėless.	
	Seneca says a good word doubtėless.	*Roman philosopher*
	He says he can no differencė find	
	Betwixt a man that is out of his mind	
495	And a man which that is drunkelew,	*drunk*
	But that woodness y-fallen in a shrew	*Except t. madness / wretch*
	Persévereth longer than does drunkenness.[1]	*Lasts*

Gluttony was the original sin in Eden

	O gluttony! full of cursedness.	
	O causė first of our confusïon![2]	
500	O original of our damnatïon,	*origin (in Eden)*
	Till Christ had bought us with His blood again!	
	Lo how dearė — shortly for to sayn —	
	A-bought was thilkė cursėd villainy.[3]	
	Corrupt was all this world for gluttony.	
505	Adam, our father, and his wife also	
	From Paradise, to labor and to woe	
	Were driven for that vice, it is no dread.	*no doubt*
	For while that Adam fasted, as I read,	
	He was in Paradise. And when that he	
510	Ate of that fruit defended on a tree,	*forbidden*
	Anon he was outcast to woe and pain.	

Exclamatio!

	O Gluttony! on thee well ought us 'plain.[4]	*complain*
	Oh, wist a man how many maladies	*Oh, if a man knew*
	Follow of excess and gluttonies,	

---

[1] 497: Seneca, the Roman philosopher, says that he can see no difference between a madman and a drunk except that the madness lasts longer.

[2] 499 ff: *our confusion:* our Fall. In this exemplum, the Original Sin that caused the Fall of mankind in Paradise was gluttony.

[3] 502-3: "Look how dearly (to state it briefly) this cursed sin was paid for *(abought)*, i.e. with Christ's blood.

[4] 512: "O Gluttony, we certainly have good reason to complain about you."

515	He wouldė be the morė measuráble	*moderate*
	Of his diet, sitting at his table.[1]	*meals*
	Alas the shortė throat, the tender mouth	
	Maketh that east and west and north and south,	
	In earth, in air, in water, men to swink	*to work*
520	To get a glutton dainty meat and drink.	*food*
	Of this matter, O Paul, well canst thou treat:[2]	*St. Paul*
	"Meat unto womb, and womb eke unto meat	*belly*
	Shall God destroyen both," as Paulus saith.	*I Cor. VI, 13.*
	Alas, a foul thing is it, by my faith	
525	To say this word, and fouler is the deed	
	When man so drinketh of the white and red	*(wines)*
	That of his throat he maketh his privy	*toilet*
	Through thilkė cursėd superfluity.	*this cursed excess*
	The Apostle weeping says full piteously:	*Phil III, 18-19.*
530	"There walken many of which you told have I	*of whom*
	(I say it now, weeping with piteous voice),	
	That they be enemies of Christė's cross,	
	Of which the end is death. Womb is their God."	*Belly,*
	O womb! O belly! O stinking cod!	*bag*
535	Fulfilled of dung and of corruptïon.	
	At either end of thee foul is the sound.	
	How greatė labour and cost is thee to find!	*to feed*
	These cookės! How they stamp and strain and grind	
	And turnen substance into accident[3]	
540	To fulfill all thy likerous talent.	*gluttonous desire*
	Out of the hardė bonės knocken they	
	The marrow, for they castė naught away	

---

[1] 515-6: *measurable / table*: the rhyme in the original Middle English probably required something like a French pronunciation and stress.

[2] 521-3: "O St Paul, you have written well on this matter (of gluttony). Food gratifies the belly and the belly enjoys the food. But both will die" (unlike the soul and spiritual food).

[3] 539: A philosophical and theological joke. In philosophy "substance" meant the "isness" of a thing, that quality that makes it what it is and not something else, and which does not change. The "accidents" are those elements of a thing, e.g. color or shape, that can change without altering its fundamental sameness. In theology this concept was used to explain how, even after the Transubstantiation of the Mass, i.e. the changing of bread and wine into the body and blood of Christ, those things did not lose the "accidents" of bread and wine. Similarly the skill of cooks could totally transform ingredients.

That may go through the gullet soft and sweet.
Of spicery, of leaf and bark and root
545   Shall be his sauce y-makèd by delight
To make him yet a newer appetite.
But certès he that haunteth such delices   *he who indulges*
Is dead while that he liveth in those vices.

Excessive drinking

A lecherous thing is wine. And drunkenness
550   Is full of striving and of wretchedness.
O drunken man, disfigured is thy face,
Sour is thy breath, foul art thou to embrace,
And through thy drunken nose seemeth the sound
As though thou saidest ay: "Samsoun! Samsoun!"   *continually*
555   And yet, God wot, Samson drank never no wine.   *God knows*
Thou fallest as it were a stickèd swine.   *stuck pig*
Thy tongue is lost, and all thine honest cure,   *self respect*
For drunkenness is very sepulture   *tomb*
Of mannè's wit, and his discretïon.   *man's intelligence*
560   In whom that drink has dominatïon
He can no counsel keep, it is no dread.   *no doubt*
Now keep you from the white and from the red,   *(wines)*
And namely from the white wine of Leap   *(in Spain)*
That is to sell in Fish Street or in Cheap.   *for sale in Cheapside*
565   This wine of Spain creepeth subtlely
In other winès growing fastè by[1]
Of which there riseth such fumosity,   *fumes*
That when a man has drunken draughtès three
And weeneth that he be at home in Cheap,   *and thinks*
570   He is in Spain, right at the town of Leap,
Not at the Rochelle nor at Bordeaux town,   *(French wine towns)*
And then will he say: 'Samsoun! Samsoun!'
But hearken, lordings, one word, I you pray
That all the sovereign actès, dare I say,   *greatest*

---

[1] 566: Chaucer, whose father was a wine-merchant near Fish St & Cheapside in London, here makes some sly reference to the illegal (?) practice of wine mixing. The Spanish wine just happens to *creep* into the wines *growing* (!) next to it. To judge from the next few lines, the mixture was very potent.

575 Of victories in the Oldė Testament,
    Through very God that is omnipotent,   *true God*
    Were done in abstinence and in prayer.
    Looketh the Bible, and there you may it lere.   *learn*

Some brief examples from the classics and Scripture

    Look Attila, the greatė conqueroúr,
580 Died in his sleep with shame and dishonoúr
    Bleeding at his nose in drunkenness.
    A captain should live in soberness.   *a general*
    And over all this aviseth you right well   *consider*
    What was commanded unto Lemuel
585 (Not Samuel, but Lemuel, say I.
    Readeth the Bible, and find it expressly)
    Of wine-giving to them that have justice.[1]
    No more of this for it may well suffice.

Gambling

    And now that I have spoke of gluttony,
590 Now will I you defenden hazardry.   *forbid gambling*
    Hazard is very mother of leasings   *Gambling / of lies*
    And of deceit and cursėd forswearings,   *perjuries*
    Blasphemy of Christ, manslaughter, and waste also
    Of chattel and of time; and furthermore   *Of goods*
595 It is reproof and contrary of honour
    For to be held a common hazarder.   *gambler*
    And ever the higher he is of estate   *rank*
    The morė is he holden desolate.   *held in contempt*
    If that a princė uses hazardry,   *gambling*
600 In allė governance and policy
    He is, as by common opinïon,
    Y-held the less in reputatïon.

Some examples from history

    Stilbon, that was a wise ambassador,
    Was sent to Corinth in full great honour

---

[1] 587: Proverbs 31, 4-5: "It is not for kings, O Lemuel, ... to drink wine ... lest they drink ... and pervert the rights of all the afflicted."

605 From Lacedaemon, to make their álliance,   *From Sparta*
     And when he came, him happenèd par chance
     That all the greatest that were of that land
     Playing at the hazard he them found.   *gambling*
     For which, as soon as that it mightè be,
610 He stole him home again to his country
     And said: "There will I not lose my name,
     Nor will not take on me so great defame
     You for to ally unto no hazarders.   *gamblers*
     Sendeth other wise ambassadors,
615 For, by my truthè, me were lever die   *I had rather*
     Than I you should to hazarders ally.   *gamblers*
     For you that be so glorious in honours
     Shall not allyen you with hazarders   *ally yourselves*
     As by my will, nor as by my treaty."   *diplomacy*
620 This wise philosopher, thus saidè he.
         Look eke that to the King Demetrius   *also*
     The King of Parthia, as the book says us,[1]
     Sent him a pair of dice of gold in scorn,
     For he had usèd hazard therebeforn
625 For which he held his glory or his renown
     At no value or reputation.
     Lords may finden other manner play   *other kinds of*
     Honest enough to drive the day away.

Swearing

     Now will I speak of oathès false and great
630 A word or two, as oldè bookès treat.
     Great swearing is a thing abominable,
     And falsè swearing is yet more reprovable.[2]
     The highè God forbade swearing at all.
     Witness on Matthew. But in speciäl   *Matt.V: 33-34*
635 Of swearing says the holy Jeremy: *Jerem. IV: 2*
     "Thou shalt swear sooth thine oathès and not lie,[3]

---

[1] 622: "The book" is John of Salisbury's *Polycraticus*, a medieval treatise on government.

[2] 631-2: As with 471-2 and elsewhere above, the original pronunciation of the rhyming words was probably closer to the French.

[3] 636-7: "You shall swear your oaths truthfully and not lie, and swear (only) in court and in rightful causes". This is not quite what modern renditions of the Jeremiah verse say.

And swear in doom and eke in rightwiseness."
But idle swearing is a cursedness.
Behold and see, that in the firstè table
640 Of Highè Godè's hestès honourable   *commandments*
How that the second hest of Him is this:
"Take not My name in idle or amiss."   *in vain*
Lo, rather, he forbiddeth such swearing
Than homicide or many a cursèd thing.[1]
645 I say that as by order thus it standeth.
This knoweth that his hestès understandeth[2]   *that = he who*
How that the second hest of God is that.   *commandment*
And furthermore, I will thee tell all plat,   *very plainly*
That vengeance shall not parten from his house
650 That of his oaths is too outragèous.
"By Godè's precious heart and by His nails
And by the blood of Christ that is in Hailes,   *Hales Abbey*
Seven is my chance, and thine is cinque and tray.   *my throw / 5 & 3*
By Godè's armès, if thou falsely play,
655 This dagger shall throughout thine heartè go."[3]
This fruit comes of the bitchèd bonès two: *cursed dice*
Forswearing, irè, falseness, homicide.   *Perjury, anger ...*
Now, for the love of Christ that for us died,
Leaveth your oathès, bothè great and small.   *Leave off*

Back to the story of the three gambling and swearing young drunks.
One of their comrades has died of the plague.

660 But, sirs, now will I tellè forth my tale.
These rioterès three, of which I tell,
Long erst ere primè rang of any bell[4]

---

[1] 643/4: "Rather" goes with "than" of the next line, i.e. "He forbids swearing rather than (ahead of) homicide." The assumption is that the Commandments in the first "table" or group — 1st, 2nd & 3rd, where the commandment against swearing occurs — are of a higher order than the other 7 where the prohibition against murder is found.

[2] 646-7: The syntax is a little snarled; the order of the phrases is as follows: "He who understands his (God's) commandments knows this: that the second commandment of God is against that (idle swearing)."

[3] 651-55: Typical profane threats of dicing gamblers. *Hailes:* an abbey in Gloucestershire, reputed to have some of Christ's blood in a vial.

[4] 662: "Long before any bell began to ring for prime" (a designated prayer hour, about 9 a.m.).

Were set them in a tavern for to drink,
And as they sat, they heard a bellė clink
665 Before a corpse was carried to his grave
That one of them 'gan callen to his knave: *his servant boy*
"Go bet," quod he "and askė readily   *Go at once / quickly*
What corpse is this that passes here forby,   *in front*
And look that thou report his namė well."
670   "Sir," quod this boy, "it needeth never a deal.   *there is no need*
It was me told ere you came here two hours.
He was, pardee, an old fellow of yours,   *by God*
And suddenly he was y-slain tonight   *last night*
Fordrunk as he sat on his bench upright.   *blind drunk*
675 There came a privy thief men clepeth Death   *stealthy thief called*
That in this country all the people slayeth
And with his spear he smote his heart in two
And went his way withouten wordės mo'.   *more*
He has a thousand slain this pestilence,   *(during) this plague*
680 And, master, ere you come in his presénce
Methinketh that it were necessary
For to beware of such an adversary.
Be ready for to meet him evermore.
Thus taughtė me my dame. I say no more."   *mother*
685   "By Saintė Mary," said this taverner,
"The child says sooth; for he has slain this year   *truth*
Hence over a mile within a great villáge
Both man and woman, child and hind and page.   *laborer & servant*
I trow his habitaïon be there.¹
690 To be advisėd great wisdom it were,   *it would be*
Ere that he did a man a dishonour."   *Before*

The young men drunkenly vow eternal
brotherhood in the quest to find Death

"Yea? Godė's armės!" quod this rioter.   *this brawler*
"Is it such peril with him for to meet?
I shall him seek by way and eke by street,   *by lane & also*
695 I make a vow, by Godė's dignė bones.   *holy*
Hearken, fellows. We three be allones.   *all one, united*

---

¹ 687: "I guess his dwelling is there".

Let each of us hold up his hand to other
And each of us become the others' brother,
And we will slay this false traitor Death.
700 He shall be slain, he that so many slayeth,
By Gode's dignity, ere it be night."
Together have these three their trothes plight *word pledged*
To live and die each of them with other
As though he were his own y-borne brother.
705 And up they start all drunken in this rage
And forth they go towards that villáge
Of which the taverner had spoke before,
And many a grisly oath then have they swore,
And Christe's blessed body they to-rent. *they tore*
710 Death shall be dead, if that they may him hent. *catch him*

They meet a mysterious old man

When they had gone not fully half a mile
Right as they would have trodden o'er a stile, *over a set of steps*
An old man and a poore with them met. *a poor old man*
This olde man full meekely them gret *greeted*
715 And saide thus: "Now, lordes, God you see."[1] *God protect you*
The proudest of these rioteres three *brawlers*
Answered again: "What, churl, with sorry grace.
Why art thou all forwrappéd save thy face? *wrapped up*
Why livest thou so long in so great age?"
720 This old man 'gan to look in his viságe,
And saide thus: "For I ne cannot find *Because I*
A man, though that I walked into Inde, *even if I w. to India*
Neither in city nor in no villáge
That woulde change his youthe for mine age,
725 And therefore must I have mine age still
As long a time as it is Gode's will.

He laments his inability to die

Nor Death, alas, ne will not have my life.
Thus walk I like a resteless caitiff, *wretch*
And on the ground, which is my mothers's gate,

---

[1] 715 ff: The courtesy of the old man who addresses the young ones as *lordes*, i.e.
gentlemen, is in marked contrast to their rudeness in addressing him as *churl*, low fellow.
What, churl, with sorry grace (717) means something like: "Hey, you lowlife, damn you."

730   I knockė with my staff both early and late,
       And sayė: 'Levė Mother, let me in.   *Dear*
       Lo how I vanish, flesh and blood and skin.
       Alas, when shall my bonės be at rest?
       Mother with you would I change my chest
735   That in my chamber longė time hath be,
       Yea, for a hairėcloth to wrappė me.'[1]
       But yet to me she will not do that grace,
       For which full pale and welkėd is my face.   *wrinkled*

He rebukes them for their lack of respect

       But, sirs, to you it is no courtesy
740   To speaken to an old man villainy   *discourtesy*
       But he trespass in word or else in deed.   *Unless he offend*
       In Holy Writ you may yourself well read   *Lev. IX, 32*
       'Against an old man, hoar upon his head
       You shall arise.'[2] Wherefore I give you redde: *stand / advice*
745   Ne do unto an old man no harm now
       No more than that you would men did to you
       In agė, if that you so long abide.   *last that long*
       And God be with you, where you go or ride.   *wherever*
       I must go thither as I have to go."   *to where*

They abuse him again, and he tells them what they want to know

750   "Nay, oldė churl, by God thou shalt not so,"
       Said this other hazarder anon.
       "Thou partest not so lightly, by Saint John.
       Thou spoke right now of thilkė traitor Death   *of this same*
       That in this country all our friendės slayeth.
755   Have here my troth as thou art his espy.   *Have ... troth = I swear / spy*
       Tell where he is or thou shalt it aby,   *suffer for*
       By God and by the Holy Sacrament,
       For soothly, thou art one of his assent   *truly*
       To slay us youngė folk, thou falsė thief."

---

[1] 736: A haircloth was a penitential garment also used as a shroud.

[2] 743-4: "In the presence of an old man with white hair upon his head,
you should stand"

760   "Now, sirs," quod he, "if that you be so lief   *so eager*
          To findė Death, turn up this crooked way,   *winding path*
          For in that grove I left him, by my fay,   *faith*
          Under a tree. And there he will abide.   *stay*
          Not for your boast he will him nothing hide.
765   See you that oak? Right there you shall him find.
          God savė you, that bought again mankind,
          And you amend."[1] Thus said this oldė man   *improve you*

In search of Death the young men find a pleasant surprise

          And ever each of these rioterės ran   *every one*
          Till he came to that tree. And there they found
770   Of florins fine of gold y-coinėd round[2]   *coins*
          Well nigh an eightė bushels, as them thought.   *nearly / it seemed to them*
          No longer then after Death they sought,
          But each of them so glad was of the sight
          For that the florins be so fair and bright
775   That down they set them by this precious hoard.
          The worst of them, he spoke the firstė word:
          "Brethren," quod he, "take keep what that I say.
          My wit is great, though that I bourd and play.   *My wisdom / joke*
          This treasure has Fortune unto us given
780   In mirth and jollity our life to liven.
          And lightly as it comes, so will we spend.
          Hey, Godė's precious dignity! Who wend   *Who (would have) thought?*
          Today that we should have so fair a grace?   *good fortune*

They plan to move their find secretly

          But might this gold be carried from this place
785   Home to mine house — or elsė unto yours,
          For well you wot that all this gold is ours —   *you know*
          Then werė we in high felicity.   *happiness*
          But truly, by day it may not be.
          Men wouldė say that we were thievės strong
790   And for our ownė treasure do us hung.   *have us hanged*
          This treasure must y-carried be by night
          As wisely and as slily as it might.

---

[1] 766-7: "May God, who redeemed mankind, save you and improve you."

[2] 770: "Round, newly minted florins (coins) of refined gold."

They agree to draw lots to decide who should go to town

Therefore I rede that cut among us all		*I advise / lots*
Be drawn, and let's see where the cut will fall,		*lot*
795 And he that has the cut, with hearté blithe		*light heart*
Shall runné to the town and that full swithe,		*quickly*
And bring us bread and wine full privily,		*secretly*
And two of us shall keepen subtlely		*discreetly*
This treasure well, and if he will not tarry,		
800 When it is night, we will this treasure carry		
By one assent where as us thinketh best."		*By agreement*
That one of them the cut brought in his fist		*lots*
And bade them draw and look where it would fall,		
And it fell on the youngest of them all,		
805 And forth toward the town he went anon.		

The two guardians of the find hatch a plot

And all so sooné as that he was gone		
That one of them spoke thus unto the other:		
"Thou knowest well thou art my sworné brother.		
Thy profit will I tell to thee anon.		
810 Thou wost well that our fellow is a-gone,		*Thou knowest*
And here is gold and that full great plenty,		
That shall departed be among us three.		*divided*
But, natheless, if I can shape it so		
That it departed were among us two,		
815 Had I not done a friendé's turn to thee?"		
That other answered: "I n'ot how that may be.		*I do not know*
He wot how that the gold is with us tway.		*He knows / us two*
What shall we do? What shall we to him say?"		
"Shall it be counsel?" said the firsté shrew,		*secret / rascal*
820 "And I shall tellen thee— in wordés few —		
What we shall do and bring it well about."		
"I granté," quod that other, "out of doubt		*I agree certainly*
That by my troth I will thee not bewray."		*betray*

The plan: treachery during a wrestling bout

"Now," quod the first, "thou wost well we be tway		*you know / two*
825 And two of us shall stronger be than one.		

Look when that he is set, thou right anon[1]
Arise, as though thou wouldest with him play,   *wrestle*
And I shall rive him through the sidès tway,   *stab*
While that thou strugglest with him as in game,
830 And with thy dagger look thou do the same,
And then shall all this gold departed be,   *divided*
My dearè friend, betwixtè thee and me.
Then may we both our lustès all fulfill   *desires*
And play at dice right at our ownè will."
835 And thus accorded been these shrewès tway   *two scoundrels*
To slay the third, as you have heard me say.

The third has a similar plan

This youngest, which that went unto the town,
Full oft in heart he rolleth up and down[2]
The beauty of these florins new and bright.
840 "O lord," quod he, "if so were that I might
Have all this treasure to myself alone,
There is no man that lives under the throne
Of God that should live so merry as I."
And at the last, the Fiend, our Enemy,   *the Devil*
845 Put in his thought that he should poison buy
With which he mightè slay his fellows tway.
For why? The Fiend found him in such living   *lifestyle*
That he had leavè him to sorrow bring.
For this was utterly his full intent
850 To slay them both, and never to repent.

He goes to the druggist

And forth he goes — no longer would he tarry —
Into the town unto a 'pothecary   *druggist*
And prayèd him that he him wouldè sell
Some poison, that he might his rattès quell.   *kill his rats*
855 And eke there was a polecat in his haw   *also / yard*
That, as he said, his capons had y-slaw,   *killed his chickens*

---

[1] 826-7: "See to it that when he sits down, you get up and pretend you want to wrestle with him."

[2] 838-9: "He continually goes over in his mind the beauty of the bright new florins."

And fain he woulde wreak him, if he might	*And gladly get revenge*
On vermin that destroyed him by night.	*On pests*
The 'pothecary answered: "And thou shalt have	*The druggist*

860 A thing that, all so God my soule save,   *all ... save = I swear*
In all this world there is no creäture
That ate or drunk has of this confiture   *concoction*
Not but the montance of a corn of wheat   *the size of a grain*
That he ne shall his life anon forlete.[1]   *promptly lose*
865 Yea, starve he shall, and that in lesse while   *shall die*
Than thou wilt go a pace not but a mile,   *a distance of only*
The poison is so strong and violent."

He borrows bottles and buys wine

This cursed man has in his hand y-hent   *taken*
This poison in a box; and sith he ran   *and then*
870 Into the nexte street unto a man,
And borrowed of him large bottles three,
And in the two his poison poured he.
The third he kepte clean for his own drink,
For all the night he shope him for to swink   *intended to work*
875 In carrying off the gold out of that place.
And when this rioter (With sorry grace!)   *Damn him (?)*
Had filled with wine his greate bottles three,
To his fellows again repaireth he.   *returns*

The denouement

What needeth it to sermon of it more?[2]
880 For right as they had cast his death before   *had planned*
Right so they have him slain and that anon.   *promptly*
And when that this was done, thus spoke that one:
"Now let us sit and drink and make us merry,
And afterwards we will his body bury."
885 And with that word it happened him *par cas*   *by chance*
To take the bottle where the poison was,

---

[1] 859 ff: The druggist promises him a poison so powerful that it is guaranteed to kill within minutes any creature that ingests an amount no bigger than a grain of wheat. *starve* in l.865 means simply to die, not here of hunger.

[2] 879: "Why make a long story of it?"

And drank, and gave his fellow drink also,
For which anon they starven bothè two.   *both died promptly*
But certès I suppose that Avicen   *certainly / Avicenna*
890 Wrote never in no Canon nor in no fen[1]
More wonder signès of empoisoning   *symptoms*
Than had these wretches two ere their ending.
Thus ended be these homicidès two   *murderers*
And eke the false empoisoner also.

Back to the sermon briefly, and to the confidence
game on the Pardoner's church audience

895 Oh cursèd sin of allè cursedness!
Oh traitors' homicide! Oh wickedness!
Oh gluttony, luxury and hazardry!   *lust & gambling*
Thou blásphemer of Christ with villainy
And oathès great of usage and of pride!
900 Alas, mankindè! How may it betide,   *How is it?*
That to thy Créator which that thee wrought   *who made you*
And with His precious heartè's blood thee bought,
Thou art so false, and so unkind, alas?
Now, good men, God forgive you your trespass,   *sin*
905 And ware you from the sin of avarice.   *beware of*
My holy pardon may you all warice,   *save*
So that you offer nobles or sterlings[2]   *gold or silver*
Or elsè silver brooches, spoonès, rings
Boweth your head under this holy bull.[3]
910 Come up, you wivès, offer of your wool.
Your names I enter here in my roll anon.
Into the bliss of heaven shall you gon.   *go*
I you assoilè by mine highè power,   *absolve*
You that will offer, as clean and eke as clear   *and also*
915 As you were born.[4]

---

[1] 889 ff: Avicenna was an Arabic philosopher and physician well known to medieval
Europe. According to Skeat, the "Canon in Medicine," his most famous work, was divided into sections called "fens."

[2] 907: "Provided you make an offering of gold or silver coins."

[3] 909: "Bull" (Lat. *bulla*, a seal) means a papal letter, almost certainly fraudulent;
hence the phrase "this holy bull" translates by chance into our vernacular as an accurate
account of the Pardoner's activity.

[4] 915: In mid line, which I have split, the Pardoner returns from the canned sermon
that he gives regularly in church, and once again address the pilgrims directly.

The Pardoner once more directly addresses his fellow pilgrims

        "And lo, sirs, thus I preach.

And Jesus Christ, that is our soulė's leech,   *physician*

So grantė you His pardon to receive,

For that is best, I will you not deceive.

But, sirs, one word forgot I in my tale:

920   I have relics and pardon in my mail   *bag*

As fair as any man in Engeland,

Which were me given by the Popė's hand.

If any of you will of devotïon

Offer, and have mine absolutïon,

925   Come forth anon and kneeleth here adown[1]

And meekėly receiveth my pardon,

Or elsė taketh pardon as you wend   *travel*

All new and fresh at every milė's end,

So that you offer always new and new   *Provided / afresh*

930   Nobles or pence which that be good and true.   *Gold coins or pennies*

He assures the pilgrims they are lucky to have him

It is an honour to ever each that is here   *to everyone*

That you may have a suffisant pardoner   *competent*

T'assoilė you in country as you ride,   *To absolve*

For áventurės which that may betide.   *accidents*

935   Peráventure, there may fall one or two   *Perhaps*

Down off his horse, and break his neck in two.

Look which a surety it is to you all[2]

That I am in your fellowship y-fall

That may assoil you, bothė more and less,   *absolve*

940   When that the soul shall from the body pass.

---

[1] 925 ff: *come, kneeleth* etc: the imperative plural form (which is also the polite singular) normally ends in *-eth*. But Chaucer's language permits dropping the *-eth*, so, as here, he uses either, depending on the form that best fits the rhythmic requirements.

[2] 937-40: "See what a good thing it is for all of you that I have chanced to be in your company, I who can absolve the rich and the poor (*more and less*), when the moment of death comes."

His joke at the Host's expense evokes a counter-joke
about the Pardoner's "relics" and his sexuality

I redé that our Host here shall begin   *I suggest*
For he is most envelopéd in sin.
Come forth, Sir Host, and offer first anon
And thou shalt kiss the relics every one,
945   Yea, for a groat. Unbuckle anon thy purse."   *groat=4 pennies*
"Nay, nay," quod he. "Then have I Christé's curse.
Let be," quod he, "it shall not be, so theech.   *I promise you*
Thou wouldest make me kiss thine oldé breech,   *underpants*
And swear it were a relic of a saint,
950   Though it were with thy fundament depaint.   *stained by y. anus*
But by that cross which that St. Helen found,
I wish I had thy collions in my hand   *testicles*
Instead of relics or of sanctuary.   *or relic box*
Let cut them off; I will thee help them carry.   *Have them cut off*
955   They shall be shrinéd in a hog's turd."[1]

The Host is surprised at the Pardoner's response

This Pardoner answered not a word.
So wroth he was, no word ne would he say.   *So angry*
"Now," quod our Host, "I will no longer play   *joke*
With thee, nor with no other angry man."

The Knight, a man of war, intervenes to restore the peace

960   But right anon the worthy Knight began
When that he saw that all the people laugh:
"No more of this, for it is right enough.
Sir Pardoner, be glad and merry of cheer,
And you, Sir Host, that be to me so dear,
965   I pray you that you kiss the Pardoner.
And Pardoner, I pray thee, draw thee near,
And as we diden, let us laugh and play."
Anon they kissed and riden forth their way.

Here is ended the Pardoner's Tale

---

[1] 952 ff: The gross sexual insult in the Host's heavy-handed joking leaves the
Pardoner speechless, perhaps for the first time in his life. The Pardoner's deficient virility
was more than hinted at in Chaucer's portrait of him in the General Prologue.

THE NUN'S PRIEST'S TALE

There is no description of the Nun's Priest in the General Prologue where we learn simply that he is a chaplain of some sort to the Prioress

Introduction

When the Monk has tired the pilgrims with his tedious narrative — a long collection of tragedies (omitted here) which could literally go on for ever because he has given them no focus — the Knight, who says he likes happy endings, calls a halt to the monotonous chronicle. The Host agrees heartily, and calls for a tale from the Nun's Priest, chaplain to the Prioress. We learn a good deal about many of the characters in *The Canterbury Tales,* including the Prioress, from *The General Prologue,* but we learn very little about the Nun's Priest there. The only mention of him is in the lines about the Prioress:

> *Another nunnė with her haddė she*
> *That was her chapelain, and priestės three (GP 163-4)*

This second nun (who is referred to confusingly, as her chaplain, i.e. her assistant) tells an unmemorable tale, but we hear no more of the other two priests. Some scholars think that the second half of line 164 here was not finished by Chaucer and was filled in by a scribe. In any case, when the Host turns to this one of the "priests three" for a more enter-taining tale, we get a little more information about the Nun's Priest who is addressed by the Host with what might seem undue familiarity. Harry Bailly, however, does this to many people with the notable exceptions of the Knight and the Prioress. Clearly the priest's job is neither prestigious nor lucrative, for he rides a nag that is both "foul and lean" and this is one reason for the innkeeper's lack of respect.

At the end of the tale we also learn that the Nun's Priest is solidly built, a virile-looking man, wasted like the Monk in a celibate profession, according to Harry. This is not much to know, all told, but it hardly matters, for we have his tale which has delighted generations of readers.

The Nun's Priest is a priest, a rather obvious statement that has a considerable bearing on the tale he tells, for priests were and are by profession preachers. And the tale that our Priest tells has a great deal in commmon with a sermon, except that it is not boring as sermons have a reputation for being.

The tale he tells is a Beast Fable, a form that dates back to the Greek of Aesop and that is still familiar in cartoons. The animals talk, discuss medicine, argue about dream theory, and so on. This is absurd and acceptable at once, though some of it is more acceptable or absurd than the rest. For example, that they should talk is acceptable enough and has been since Aesop, but that the hen should comment on the absence of a local drugstore where one could get laxatives, and that her "husband" should quote Cato and discuss predestination is deliciously daft.

One of the subjects that the animals talk about is the significance of dreams — a favorite subject of Chaucer's, who wrote a good deal of "Dream Poetry," a very common medieval form. In the Dream Vision the author generally portrays himself as falling asleep, and the poem is a report of what he dreamed. But Chaucer was also interested in the *theory* of dreams, and the discussion between the cock and the hen in the tale represents well enough the differing points of view in the Middle Ages about the origin and significance of dreams. (See also Select Glossary)

The argument is carried on to a sizeable degree by a common medieval method — the "exemplum." The exemplum is an anecdote ranging from very brief to extended, told to illustrate the point being made in an argument or in a sermon (and the teller of this tale is, as we have said, a priest). There is a string of these *exempla* in this tale: biblical references of one or two lines each, a passage of around eighty lines about the two travelling salesmen; stories from folklore, English or Old Testament history and the Latin classics. These were "authorities," that is, authoritative sources adduced to bolster the assertions of the speaker or writer. The people of the Middle Ages believed greatly in "authorities" .

Another topic favored by Chaucer and much argued in the Middle Ages, but somehow a good deal less plausible in this context and hence perhaps more comic, is the problem of Free Will, that is, the difficulty of reconciling man's free will with God's omniscience. If you do something, do you do it because you were really free to do it, or did you *have* to do it? Since God in His omniscience foresaw from all eternity that you would or would not do it, does that imply that you were not free to choose in the first place? Is free will a delusion?

Since this argument generally occurred in the context of discussion about sin and eternal salvation, it was a deeply serious matter for many people. Introducing such a problem into a barnyard squabble between a cock and a hen is comic, but it does not dismiss the topic as ridiculous in itself, just as it does not reduce the literary or historical significance of the Fall of Troy or the burning of Carthage because they are comically compared to the goings on in the widow's barnyard.

There are other forms of humor embedded in the tale, some of them less obvious than comparing the seizure of a cock by a fox to the Fall of Man or the Fall of Troy. The humor depends upon the reader's recognition of some features of medieval rhetoric, such as *exclamatio* to express great emotion, recommended especially by one book well known to Chaucer and his contemporaries, Geoffrey (or Gaufred) de Vinsauf's *Poetria Nova*. But the three passages of "exclamation" have a mock epic quality obvious enough even without knowledge of de Vinsauf's work.

Like most beast fables *The Nun's Priest's Tale* ends with a moral, in this case for anyone who trusts in flattery and for him who "jangles when he should hold his peace." Take the morality, good men. Or, to put it another way, "take the fruit and let the chaff be still." The reader will have to decide which is which.

PROLOGUE TO
THE NUN'S PRIEST'S TALE

The Knight interrupts the Monk's Tale , a string of tragedies.

	"Whoa!" quod the Knight. "Good sir, no more of this.	*said the K.*
	What you have said, is right enough y-wis,	*indeed*
	And muchel more. For little heaviness	*much*
3960	Is right enough to muchel folk, I guess.	*most people*
	I say for me, it is a great dis-ease,	*distress*
	Where as men have been in great wealth and ease,	
	To hearen of their sudden fall, alas!	
	And the contrary is joy and great soláce,	
3965	As when a man has been in poor estate,	
	And climbeth up, and waxeth fortunate,	*grows, becomes*
	And there abideth in prosperity.	
	Such thing is gladsome, as it thinketh me,	*it seems to me*
	And of such thing were goodly for to tell."	

The Host agrees.

	"Yea," quod our Host, "by Sainté Paulé's bell	*said our Host*
3970	You say right sooth; this monk he clappeth loud	*You speak truth*
	He spoke how Fortune covered with a cloud	
	I n'ot never what, and also of tragedy	*I know not*
	Right now you heard; and, pardee, no remedy	*by God*
3975	It is for to bewail, nor to complain	
	That that is done, and also 'tis a pain,	*That which*
	As you have said, to hear of heaviness.	
	Sir Monk, no more of this, so God you bless.	
	Your tale annoyeth all this company;	
3980	Such talking is not worth a butterfly,	
	For therein is there no desport nor game.	*no fun*

Wherefore, Sir Monk, Daun Piers by your name,
I pray you heartily, tell us somewhat else,
For sikerly, n'ere clinking of your bells,   *certainly were it not*
3985   That on your bridle hang on every side,
By heaven's king, that for us allė died,
I should ere this have fallen down for sleep,
Although the slough had never been so deep.   *mud*
Then had your talė all been told in vain.
3990   For certainly, as that these clerkės sayn,   *scholars*
Where as a man may have no audience,
Nought helpeth it to tellen his sentence.[1]   *story, opinion*
And well I wot the substance is in me,   *I know*
If anything shall well reported be.
3995   Sir, say somewhat of hunting, I you pray."
"Nay," quod this Monk, "I have no lust to play. *no desire / be amusing*
Now let another tell as I have told."

The Host turns to the Prioress's chaplain

Then spoke our Host with rudė speech and bold   *rough speech*
And said unto the Nunnė's Priest anon:
4000   "Come near, thou Priest, come hither, thou Sir John,[2]
Tell us such thing as may our heartės glad.   *gladden*
Be blithė, though thou ride upon a jade.   *Be happy / nag*
What though thine horse be bothė foul and lean   *dirty and skinny*
If he will serve thee, reckė not a bean.   *do not care*
4005   Look that thine heart be merry evermo."
"Yes, sir," quod he, "yes, Host, so may I go,
But I be merry, y-wis I will be blamed."   *Unless I'm m., indeed*
And right anon his tale he has attamed,   *started*
And thus he said unto us every one,
4010   This sweetė priest, this goodly man, Sir John.

---

[1] 3992-4 *Where as ... reported be:* "There is no point in telling your story when no one is listening. I do know a good story when I hear one.(?)"

[2] 4000 "Sir John" is not a title of knighthood, but a less respectful way of designating a priest than the title of "Daun" applied to the Monk (see Endpapers). The priest's job as chaplain to the Prioress is not important enough to evoke the innkeeper's respect.

THE NUN'S PRIEST'S TALE

The contented life of a poor country widow

A poore widow somedeal stape in age — *somewhat advanced*
Was whilom dwelling in a narrow cottáge, — *once upon a time*
Beside a grove, standing in a dale.
This widow, of which I telle you my tale,
4015 Since thilke day that she was last a wife, — *that day*
In patience led a full simple life,
For little was her chattel and her rent. — *property & income*
By husbandry of such as God her sent — *by thrift*
She found herself, and eke her daughters two. — *supported / & also*
4020 Three large sowes had she, and no mo', — *more*
Three kine, and eke a sheep that highte Mall. — *cows / was called*
Full sooty was her bower, and eke her hall, — *bedroom / and also*
In which she ate full many a slender meal.
Of poignant sauce her needed never a deal. — *sharp / not at all*
4025 No dainty morsel passed through her throat;
Her diet was accordant to her cote. — *coat (or cottage)*
Repletion ne made her never sick; — *Gluttony*
A temperate diet was all her physic, — *her medicine*
And exercise, and hearte's suffisance. — *peace of mind*
4030 The goute let her nothing for to dance, — *did not hinder from*
No apoplexy shente not her head. — *gave her headaches*
No wine ne drank she, neither white nor red.
Her board was served most with white and black — — *table*
Milk and brown bread — in which she found no lack,
4035 Seynd bacon, and sometime an egg or tway; — *smoked bacon / or 2*
For she was as it were a manner dey. — *kind of dairy-woman ?*

One animal in her yard was a splendid rooster

A yard she had, enclosed all about
With sticks, and a dry ditch without, — *outside*
In which she had a cock hight Chanticleer, — *rooster called*
4040 In all the land of crowing n'as his peer. — *he had no equal*
His voice was merrier than the merry organ,
On masse days that in the churche gon. — *goes, plays*

Well sikerer was his crowing in his lodge,   *More dependable*
Than is a clock, or any abbey orloge.   *abbey bell*
4045   By nature he knew each ascensïon
Of the equinoctial in thilkė town;[1]
For when degrees fifteenė were ascended,
Then crew he, that it might not be amended.   *improved*
His comb was redder than the fine coral,
4050   And battled, as it were a castle wall.
His bill was black, and as the jet it shone;
Like azure were his leggės and his tone;   *toes*
His nails whiter than the lily flower,
And like the burnėd gold was his coloúr.[2]

The cock's favorite wife, Pertelote

4055   This gentle cock had in his governance
Seven hens, for to do all his pleasánce,   *his pleasure*
Which were his sisters and his paramours,   *lovers*
And wonder like to him, as of coloúrs.
Of which the fairest-huėd on her throat,   *prettiest-colored*
4060   Was clepėd fairė Damoiselle Pertelote.[3]   *was called*
Courteous she was, discreet, and debonair,   *gracious*
And compaignable, and bore herself so fair,   *sociable, & conducted*
Since thilkė day that she was sevennights old   *a week*
That truly she has the heart in hold
4065   Of Chanticleer, lockėd in every lith.   *limb*
He loved her so, that well was him therewith.   *he was totally happy*
But such a joy it was to hear them sing,
When that the brightė sun began to spring,
In sweet accord, "My lief is fare in land."   *My love has gone away*
4070   For thilkė time, as I have understand   *at that time*
Beastės and birdės couldė speak and sing.

---

[1] 4045-8 *By nature ... amended:* He knew the exact time of day from observing the sun in the sky above him. He kept exact clock time; 15 degrees of equinoctial measure was one hour. Chaucer is inordinately fond of this kind of astro-jargon.

[2] 4054 *His comb ... colour:* In their edition of the tale Coghill and Tolkien assure us that this is a good description of a cock of the Golden Spangled Hamburg breed.

[3] 4060 *Damoiselle* should probably be pronounced "damsel".

Chanticleer has a terrible dream

And so befell, that in a dawening   *At dawn*
As Chanticleer among his wivės all
Sat on his perchė that was in the hall,
4075 And next him sat this fairė Pertelote;
This Chanticleer gan groanen in his throat,
As man that in his dream is dretchėd sore   *much troubled*
And when that Pertelote thus heard him roar,
She was aghast, and said: "O heartė dear,   *afraid*
4080 What aileth you to groan in this mannėr?
You be a very sleeper, fie for shame!"
And he answered and saidė thus: "Madame,
I pray you that you take it not a-grief.   *badly*
By God, me mett I was in such mischief   *I dreamt / such trouble*
4085 Right now, that yet mine heart is sore affright.
Now God," quod he, "my sweven rede aright,[1]
And keep my body out of foul prisoún.
Me mett how that I roamėd up and down   *I dreamed*
Within our yard, where as I saw a beast,
4090 Was like a hound, and would have made arrest
Upon my body, and have had me dead.
His colour was betwixtė yellow and red;
And tippėd was his tail, and both his ears
With black, unlike the remnant of his hairs.
4095 His snoutė small, with glowing eyen tway.   *eyes two*
Yet of his look for fear almost I die.
This causėd me my groaning doubtėless."

Pertelote is shocked and disappointed

"Avoy!" quod she, "fie on you, heartless.[2]   *"Out!" / faintheart*
Alas!" quod she, "for by that God above
4100 Now have you lost my heart and all my love;
I cannot love a coward, by my faith.

---

[1] 4086 *Now God ... aright:* "May God make my dream come out the right way." *Me mette ...* is the impersonal use of the obsolete verb, meaning literally "it was dreamed to me," or "I dreamt". It is also used with the usual modern order: *he mette. Dream* is used as both verb and noun, but *sweven* only as noun.

[2] 4098 *Avoy* and *fie* both mean someting like *Shame!*

For certès, what so any woman saith,   *no matter what*
We all desiren, if it mightè be,
To havè husbands, hardy, wise, and free,   *brave, wise, generous*
4105 And secret, and no niggard nor no fool,   *discreet & no skinflint*
Nor him that is aghast of every tool,
Nor no avaunter, by that God above.   *no boaster*
How durst you say for shame unto your love   *How dare you*
That anything might maken you afeared?
4110 Have you no man's heart, and have a beard?

Her diagnosis and prescription of home remedies

Alas! and can you be aghast of swevenès?   *afraid of dreams*
Nothing, God wot, but vanity in sweven is.   *God knows / nonsense*
"Swevens engender of repletïons,[1]
And oft of fumes and of complexïons
4115 When humours be too abundant in a wight.[2]   *in a person*
Certès this dream which you have mett tonight
Comes of the greatè superfluity
Of yourè reddè cholerè, pardee,   *red bile, by God*
Which causeth folk to dreaden in their dreams
4120 Of arrows, and of fire with reddè lemes,   *red light*
Of reddè beastès, that they will them bite,
Of conteke, and of whelpès great and lite;   *fighting / dogs / little*
Right as the humour of meláncholy[3]
Causeth full many a man in sleep to cry,
4125 For fear of blackè bears or bullès black
Or else that blackè devils will them take.
Of other humours could I tell also,
That worken many a man in sleep full woe,
But I will pass, as lightly as I can.
4130 Lo Cato, which that was so wise a man,[4]

---

[1] 4113: "Dreams are caused by excess" (of eating and drinking). There was a good deal of speculation and theorizing about dreams before and during the Middle Ages. Chaucer himself was especially interested in the subject. See Select Glossary.

[2] 4115: See Select Glossary under "Humor" for explanation of "humor" and "complexion," the forces in the body that were supposed to account for sickness, health, good or bad disposition.

[3] 4123 Melancholy was supposed to be caused by black bile.

[4] 4130: Cato was the supposed author of "Distichs," a book of Latin maxims commonly used in schools.

Said he not thus: 'Ne do no force of dreams'? *Pay no heed*
Now, Sir," quod she, "when we fly from the beams,
For Godė's love, as take some laxative.
On peril of my soul, and of my life,
4135 I counsel you the best, I will not lie,
That both of choler, and of melancholy
You purgė you; and for you shall not tarry, *purge yourself / delay*
Though in this town is no apothecary, *pharmacist*
I shall myself to herbės teachen you, *about herbs*
4140 That shall be for your health, and for your prow; *profit,*
And in our yard those herbės shall I find,
The which have of their property by kind *natural properties*
To purgen you beneath, and eke above.
Forget not this for Godė's ownė love.
4145 You be full choleric of complexïon.
Beware the sun in his ascensïon *noonday sun*
Ne find you not replete of humours hot, *full of*
And if it do, I dare well lay a groat, *bet a dollar*
That you shall have a fever tertïane,[1]
4150 Or an ague that may be your bane. *illness / death*
A day or two you shall have digestives
Of wormės, ere you take your laxatives,
Of laureole, centaury, and fumetere, *medicinal herbs*
Or else of hellėbore that groweth there,
4155 Of catapuce, or of gaitre-berries, *more herbs*
Or herb ivy growing in our yard, there merry 'tis
Pick them right up as they grow, and eat them in.
Be merry, husband, for your father's kin. *for goodness sake*
Dreadeth no dream. I can say you no more."

Chanticleer's justification of the value of dreams

4160 "Madame," quod he, "gramercy of your lore. *thanks for advice*
But natheless, as touching Daun Catoun. *Cato*
That has of wisdom such a great renown,
Though that he bade no dreamės for to dread,
By God, men may in olden bookės read,
4165 Of many a man, more of authority

---

[1] 4149 *fever tertiane:* A fever that peaked every third day, or every other day by our reckoning.

Than ever Cato was, so may I thee,   *so may I thrive*
That all the reverse say of this senténce,   *opinion*
And have well founden by experience,
That dreamės be signíficatïons
4170   As well of joy as tríbulatïons
That folk enduren in this life presént.
There needeth make of this no argument;

An anecdote that proves the importance of dreams

The very proofė showeth it indeed.   *actual experience*
One of the greatest authors that men read,
4175   Says thus: that whilom two fellows went   *that once 2 comrades*
On pilgrimage in a full good intent;   *On a journey*
And happened so, they came into a town,
Where as there was such congregatïon   *such a crowd*
Of people, and eke so strait of herbergage,   *shortage of rooms*
4180   That they ne found as much as one cottáge,
In which they mightė both y-lodgėd be.
Wherefore they mustė—of necessity,
As for that night—departen company;   *part company*
And each of them goes to his hostelry,
4185   And took his lodging as it wouldė fall.   *he could get it*
That one of them was lodgėd in a stall,   *stable*
Far in a yard, with oxen of the plough;
That other man was lodgėd well enow,   *enough*
As was his áventure, or his fortúne   *luck or fate*
4190   That us govérneth all, as in commune.   *all together*
   And so befell, that, long ere it were day,
This man mett in his bed, there as he lay,
How that his fellow gan upon him call,   *his companion*
And said: 'Alas! for in an ox's stall
4195   This night shall I be murdered, where I lie,
Now help me, dearė brother, or I die;
In allė hastė come to me,' he said.
This man out of his sleep for fear abraid,   *awoke*
But when that he was wakened of his sleep,
4200   He turnėd him, and took of this no keep;   *turned over / no heed*
Him thought his dream was but a vanity.   *a delusion*
Thus twicė in his sleeping dreamėd he.

And at the thirdė time yet his fellow
Came, as him thought, and said, 'I am now slaw.   *slain*
4205 Behold my bloody woundės, deep and wide.
Arise up early, in the morrow tide,   *in the morning*
And at the west gate of the town,' quod he,
'A cartė full of dung there shalt thou see,
In which my body is hid full privily.   *secretly*
4210 Do thilkė cart arresten boldély.[1]
My goldė caused my murder, sooth to sayn.'   *truth to say*
And told him every point how he was slain
With a full piteous facė, pale of hue.   *of color*
And trusteth well, his dream he found full true;
4215 For on the morrow, as soon as it was day,
To his fellow's inn he took the way,
And when that he came to this ox's stall,
After his fellow he began to call.   *For his companion*
The hosteler answérėd him anon,   *hotel owner*
4220 And saidė: 'Sir, your fellow is agone;
As soon as day he went out of the town.'
This man gan fallen in suspicïon,
Remembering on his dreamės that he mett,   *dreamed*
And forth he goes, no longer would he let,   *delay*
4225 Unto the west gate of the town, and found
A dung cart — as it were to dung the land —
That was arrayėd in that samė wise
As you have heard the deadė man devise.   *tell*
And with a hardy heart he gan to cry
4230 Vengeance and justice of this felony:
'My fellow murdered is this samė night,
And in this cart he lies, gaping upright.
I cry out on the ministers,' quod he,   *officials*
'That shouldė keep and rulen this city.   *administer*
4235 Harrow! Alas! here lies my fellow slain.'   *(Cries of dismay)*
What should I more unto this talė sayn?
The people out start, and cast the cart to ground,
And in the middle of the dung they found
The deadė man, that murdered was all new.   *recently*

---

[1] 4210 *Do thilke...:* "Have this cart stopped."

Exclamatio!

4240   O blissful God! that art so just and true,
       Lo, how that thou bewrayest murder alway.   *revealest*
       Murder will out, that see we day by day.
       Murder is so wlatsom and abominable   *nasty*
       To God, that is so just and reasonable,
4245   That he ne will not suffer it helėd be.   *allow to be hid*
       Though it abide a year, or two, or three,
       Murder will out, this is my conclusion.[1]
       And right anon, the ministers of the town
       Have hent the carter, and so sore him pined,   *tortured*
4250   And eke the hosteler so sore engíned,   *racked*
       That they beknew their wickedness anon,   *confessed*
       And were a-hangėd by the neckė bone.

Another anecdote about dreams

       Here may men see that dreamės be to dread.   *to be feared*
       And certės in the samė book I read,
4255   Right in the nextė chapter after this,
       (I gabbė not, so have I joy and bliss),
       Two men that would have passėd o'er the sea
       For certain cause, into a far country,
       If that the wind ne had been contrary,
4260   That made them in a city for to tarry,
       That stood full merry upon an haven side.   ·   *near the harbor*
       But on a day, against the eventide,   *towards evening*
       The wind gan change, and blew right as them lest.   *as they wanted*
       Jolly and glad they went unto their rest,
4265   And casten them full early for to sail.   *planned*
          But to that one man fell a great marvail.   *marvel*
       That one of them in sleeping as he lay,
       Him mett a wonder dream, against the day: *dreamt / near dawn*
       Him thought a man stood by his beddė's side

---

[1] 4247 *O blisful God … conclusion:* This passage sounds a great deal more like a
preacher than a rooster. Some medieval scribe wrote in the margin "Auctor" (Author), i.e.
he saw that the narrator (the priest) rather than the rooster was bursting through the
already thin fiction and delivering the kind of exclamation expected of an "auctoritee,"
someone who made sententious statements.

4270 And him commanded that he should abide,	*stay*
And said him thus: 'If thou to-morrow wend,	*go, travel*
Thou shalt be drowned; my tale is at an end.'	
He woke, and told his fellow what he mett,	*dreamt*
And prayèd him his voyage for to let,	*to delay*
4275 As for that day, he prayed him to abide.	
His fellow, that lay by his beddè's side,	
Gan for to laugh, and scornèd him full fast.	
'No dream,' quod he, 'may so my heart aghast,	*terrify*
That I will letten for to do my things.	*delay*
4280 I settè not a straw by thy dreamings,	
For swevens be but vanities and japes.	*dreams / nonsense*
Men dream all day of owlès and of apes,	*every day*
And eke of many a mazè therewithal;	*fantastic things*
Men dream of thing that never was, nor shall.	
4285 But since I see that thou wilt here abide,	
And thus forslothen wilfully thy tide,	*deliberately waste time*
God wot it rueth me, and have good day.'	*God knows, I'm sorry*
And thus he took his leave, and went his way.	
But ere that he had half his course y-sailed,	
4290 N'ot I not why, nor what mischance it ailed,	*I don't know*
But casually the ship's bottom rent,	*by chance / tore*
And ship and man under the water went	
In sight of other shippès it beside	
That with them sailèd at the samè tide.	*time*

Chanticleer's triumphant conclusion from these examples

4295 And therefore, fairè Pertelote so dear,	
By such examples old yet mayst thou lere	*learn*
That no man shouldè be too reckèless	*contemptuous*
Of dreams, for I say thee doubtèless,	
That many a dream full sore is for to dread.	

Another briefer anecdote

4300 Lo, in the life of Saint Kenélm I read,	
That was Kenulphus' son, the noble king	
Of Mercenrike, how Kénelm mett a thing.[1]	*dreamt*

---

[1] 4302 *Lo ... Mercenrike:* The syntax here is awkward: "I read in the life of St. Kenelm, the son of Kenulph who was the noble king of Mercia ...." Notice that the name Kenelm is stressed differently on one line than on the other. Mercia was a part of England in the days when it was still divided into a number of kingdoms.

A little ere he were murdered on a day,
His murder in his visïon he say.   *saw*
4305   His nurse to him expounded every deal   *every bit*
His sweven, and bade him for to keep him well   *guard himself*
From treason. But he n'as but seven years old,   *was only*
And therefore little talë has he told   *attention he paid*
Of any dream, so holy was his heart.
4310   By God, I haddë lever than my shirt,   *I had rather*
That you had read his legend, as have I.   *his biography*
Dame Pertelote, I say you truly,
Macrobius, that wrote the visïon   *dream*
In Afric' of the worthy Scipion,
4315   Affirmeth dreams, and sayeth that they be
Warning of thingës that men after see.[1]

A series of shorter examples of dreams that foretold disaster

And furthermore, I pray you looketh well
In the Old Testament, of Danïel,   *Book of Daniel*
If he held dreams of any vanity.[2]
4320   Read eke of Joseph, and there shall you see
Whether dreams be sometimes (I say not all)
Warning of thingës that shall after fall.
Look of Egypt the king, Daun Pharaoh,
His baker and his butler also,
4325   Whether they feltë no effect in dreams.   *Gen 37 to 41*
Whoso will seeken acts of sundry reams,   *realms, kingdoms*
May read of dreamës many a wonder thing.
    Lo Croesus, which that was of Lydia king,   *who was king of L.*
Mett he not that he sat upon a tree,   *Dreamt*
4330   Which signified he should a-hangëd be?
Lo here, Andromache, Hector's wife,   *H., hero of Troy*
That day that Hector shouldë lose his life,
She dreamëd on the samë night beforn,
How that the life of Hector should be lorn,
4335   If thilkë day he went into battail.   *battle*

---

[1] 4314-6 Macrobius wrote a book well known in the Middle Ages, a *Commentary* on Cicero's *Dream of Scipio*, i.e. the Scipio known as Scipio Africanus because of his defeat of Hannibal in Africa. Macrobius was the source of much medieval theory about dreams.

[2] 4319 "If he considered dreams to be just nonsense or delusion."

She warnèd him, but it might not avail;
He wentè for to fightè natheless,
And was y-slain anon of Achilles.   *killed by A.*
But thilkè tale is all too long to tell,
4340 And eke it is nigh day, I may not dwell.   *near day / go on*
Shortly I say, as for conclusïon,
That I shall have of this avisïon
Adversity; and I say furthermore,
That I ne tell of laxatives no store,   *have no time for*
4345 For they be venomous, I wot it well.   *I know*
I them defy, I love them never a deal.

*But let us think of more pleasurable things — and **do** them*

Now let us speak of mirth, and stint all this.   *and stop*
Madame Pertelote, so have I bliss,
Of one thing God has sent me largè grace,
4350 For when I see the beauty of your face,
You be so scarlet red about your eyen,   *eyes*
It maketh all my dreadè for to dien,
For, all so siker as *"In principio,"*   *sure as Gospel*
Mulier est hominis confusio.[1]
4355 (Madam, the sentence of this Latin is,   *the meaning, sense*
Woman is man's joy and all his bliss).
For when I feel a-night your softè side,
Albeit that I may not on you ride,
For that our perch is made so narrow, alas!
4360 I am so full of joy and of soláce,
That I defy bothè sweven and dream."[2]

He finds a better remedy for fear than laxatives

And with that word he flew down from the beam;
For it was day, and eke his hennès all;

---

[1] 4354 *In principio* are the first words of St. John's gospel: *In the beginning* was the word ... The phrase was used either as a blessing or for something like "the gospel truth." *Mulier est hominis confusio* means "Woman is man's ruination," but it is deliberately mistranslated, as a little male insiders' joke. The priest (and perhaps Chanticleer) know Latin, and know that Pertelote and the Prioress do not. Priest and rooster want to have their joke *and* keep their jobs, as servants either of Venus or of Diana.

[2] 4361 Some difference between "sweven" and "dream" seems to be intended, but it is not clear what.

And with a chuck he gan them for to call,
4365 For he had found a corn lay in the yard.
Royal he was, he was no more afeared.   *R = like a king*
He feathered Pertelotė twenty time,   *mounted*
And trod her eke as oft ere it was prime.   *rode / also / 9 a.m.*
He looketh as it were a grim lion;
4370 And on his toes he roameth up and down,
Him deignėd not to set his feet to ground.
He chucketh, when he has a corn y-found,   *clucks*
And to him runnen then his wivės all.

The sun's in the heavens; all's right with his world

Thus royal, as a prince is in his hall,
4375 Leave I this Chanticleer in his pastúre;
And after will I tell his áventure.   *what happened*
    When that the month in which the world began,
That hightė March, when God first makėd man,   *[a medieval belief]*
Was complete, and passėd were also
4380 Since March be gone, thirty days and two,   *ended / i.e. on May 3*
Befell that Chanticleer in all his pride,
His seven wivės walking by his side
Cast up his eyen to the brighte sun,
That in the sign of Taurus had y-run
4385 Twenty degrees and one, and somewhat more
He knew by kind, and by none other lore,   *by instinct / learning*
That it was prime, and crew with blissful steven: *9 a.m. / voice*
"The sun," he said, "is clomben up on heaven   *has climbed*
Forty degrees and one, and more y-wis.   *Indeed*
4390 Madámė Pertelote, my worldė's bliss,
Hearkeneth these blissful birdės — how they sing!
And see the freshė flowers — how they spring!
Full is mine heart of revel, and soláce."

But ...

But suddenly him fell a sorrowful case,   *to him happened*
4395 For ever the latter end of joy is woe.
God wot that worldly joy is soon ago,   *God knows / gone*
And if a rhetor couldė fair endite,   *rhetorician / write*
He in a chronicle safely might it write,

As for a sovereign notability.   *basic principle*
4400 Now every wise man let him hearken me.
This story is as true, I undertake
As is the book of Launcelot du Lake,
That women hold in full great reverence.[1]
Now will I turn again to my senténce.   *story, sermon*

A crafty but wicked creature has stolen into this Paradise

4405 A coal fox, full of sly iniquity,
That in the grove had wonèd yearès three,   *had lived*
By high imaginatïon forecast,[2]
The samè night throughout the hedges brast   *burst*
Into the yard where Chanticleer the fair
4410 Was wont, and eke his wivès, to repair;   *accustomed / to go*
And in a bed of wortès still he lay,   *cabbages or weeds*
Till it was passèd undern of the day,   *mid-morning*
Waiting his time on Chanticleer to fall,
As gladly do these homicidès all,
4415 That in awaitè lie to murder men.

Exclamatio!

O false murderer! lurking in thy den!
O new Iscariot, new Ganelon!
O false dissimuler, O Greek Sinon,
That broughtest Troy all utterly to sorrow![3]
4420 O Chanticleer! accursed be that morrow
That thou into that yard flew from the beams.
Thou wert full well y-warnèd by thy dreams,
That thilkè day was perilous to thee.

---

[1] 4403 Lancelot of the Lake was a prominent hero of Arthurian legend, a great warrior, and a great lover—of Queen Guinevere. This rather sarcastic statement is possibly another jab at his employer.

[2] 4407 *By high ...:* This line presumably means to suggest that the fox breaking through the fence was something foreseen by the *high imagination* of God himself.

[3] 4419 Judas Iscariot betrayed Jesus Christ; Ganelon was a French traitor in *The Song of Roland*; Sinon betrayed Troy. The absurdly inflated comparisons in the impassioned exclamation are meant to mock the practice of some preachers and the recommendations of some rhetoricians like Geoffrey of Vinsauf.

A theological question: Do we have Free Will or not?

But what that God forewot must needės be,	*foreseees has to be*
4425 After the opinïon of certain clerkės.[1]	
Witness on him that any perfect clerk is,	*any good scholar*
That in school is great altercatïon	*argument*
In this mattér, and great disputatïon,	
And has been of an hundred thousand men.	
4430 But I ne cannot bolt it to the bren,	*sift it / bran*
As can the holy doctor Augustine,	*teacher St. Augustine*
Or Boece, or the bishop Bradwardine,	*Boethius*
Whether that Godė's worthy forewitting	*foreknowledge*
Straineth me needfully to do a thing,	*Compels me of necessity*
4435 (Needly clepe I simple necessity)	
Or elsė if free choice be granted me	
To do that samė thing, or do it not,	
Though God forewot it ere that it was wrought	*knew before / done*
Or if his witting straineth never a deal,	*knowing compels not*
4440 But by necessity conditional.	

But this is too abstruse

I will not have to do of such mattér.[2]	
My tale is of a cock, as you may hear,	
That took his counsel of his wife with sorrow	*advice / unfortunately*
To walken in the yard upon that morrow	
4445 That he had mett that dream that I of told.	*dreamt*
Women's counsels be full often cold;	*women's advice*
Woman's counsel brought us first to woe,	
And made Adam out of Paradise to go,	
There as he was full merry, and well at ease.	
4450 But for I n'ot to whom it might displease,	*because I know not*
If I counsel of women wouldė blame,	
Pass over, for I said it in my game.	*as a joke*

---

[1] 4425 *After the opinion* ...: "According to the opinion of certain scholars what God forsees must come to pass." The thorny question of reconciling man's free will and God's omniscience had been dealt with famously by St Augustine of Hippo, by Boethius in *The Consolations of Philosophy,* and by Bishop Bradwardine, an English scholar.

[2] 4441: The NP says that he will have nothing to do with such abstruse matters, although he has touched on them in such a way as to indicate that he knows a good deal about them, distinguishing, for example, between "simple necessity" and "necessity conditional," terms devised by Boethius in his philosophical argument.

Read authors, where they treat of such mattér,
And what they say of woman you may hear.
4455   These be the cocké's wordés, and not mine;
I can no harm of no woman divine.[1]

Back from these abstractions to the story.
Chanticleer suddenly sees the enemy.

Fair in the sand, to bathe her merrily,
Lies Pertelote, and all her sisters by,
Against the sun, and Chanticleer so free   *In the sun*
4460   Sang merrier than the mermaid in the sea,
For Physiologus says sikerly,   *certainly*
How that they singen well and merrily.[2]
And so befell that as he cast his eye
Among the wortes on a butterfly,   *cabbages, weeds*
4465   He was 'ware of this fox that lay full low.
Nothing ne list him then for to crow,   *Not at all inclined*
But cried anon "Cock! cock!" and up he start,
As man that was affrayéd in his heart.   *frightened*
For naturally a beast desireth flee
4470   From his contráry, if he may it see,
Though he ne'er erst had seen it with his eye.   *never before*

The fox's smooth seduction tactic: he praises
the singing of Chanticleer and his father

This Chanticleer, when he gan him espy,
He would have fled, but that the fox anon
Said: "Gentle Sir, alas! what will you don?   *do*
4475   Be you afraid of me that am your friend?
Now certés, I were worsé than a fiend,   *any devil*
If I to you would harm or villainy.   *wished*

---

[1] 4456 "I can discover no harm in women"; *divine* is a verb meaning something like "discover, find"; but there might be wordplay on *divine*, an adjective coming after its noun, and meaning "religious woman," like the Prioress, his employer. The whole second half of the passage beginning *But for I n'ot ...* seems to be the Priest's scramble to undo the effect of his lapse into the common medieval preacher's anti feminist charge in the preceding lines.

[2] 4462 *Physiologus* is a bestiary, a book about Natural History giving information, much of it very fanciful, about animals. *Sikerly* is not a good word to describe the science displayed in bestiaries.

I am not come your counsel for to spy   *your secrets*
But truly the cause of my coming
4480 Was only for to hearken how you sing,
For truly you have as merry a steven.   *voice*
As any angel has that is in heaven;
Therewith you have in music more feeling,   *Besides*
Than had Boece, or any that can sing.[1]
4485 My lord your father (God his soulė bless)
And eke your mother of her gentleness
Have in mine house y-been, to my great ease:[2]
And certės, Sir, full fain would I you please.
But for men speak of singing, I will say,[3]
4490 So may I brooken well mine eyen tway,   *as I hope to enjoy*
Save you, ne heard I never man yet sing   *Besides you*
As did you father in the morwening.   *morning*
Certės it was of heart all that he sung.
And for to make his voice the morė strong,
4495 He would so pain him, that with both his eyen   *take pains*
He mustė wink, so loudė would he crien,   *shut his eyes*
And standen on his tiptoes therewithal,   *as well*
And stretchen forth his neckė long and small.
And eke he was of such discretïon,
4500 That there was no man in no regïon,
That him in song or wisdom might surpass.
     I have well read in Daun Burnel the ass   *(in the story of)*
Among his verse, how that there was a cock,
For that a priestė's son gave him a knock
4505 Upon his leg, while he was young and nice,   *and foolish*
He made him for to lose his benefice.[4]   *parish*
But certain there is no comparison

---

[1] 4484 Boece is Boethius, the philosopher we have heard about already, who also had written on music. See also note to 4425 above.

[2] 4487 *your father ... ease*: The implication is that he has eaten both of them.

[3] 4489 *But for men speak ...*: "But when it comes to talking about singing, I will say, (I swear by my eyes) that with the exception of yourself, I never heard a better singer than your father in the mornings."

[4] 4506 In the story of Burnell the Ass, a satiric poem, one incident relates how a cock got his revenge on a man who was to be made priest and get a parish (benefice). The cock refused to crow on time, so the man failed to get to the ordination ceremony, and so lost the parish.

Betwixt the wisdom and discretïon
Of your father, and of his subtlety.
4510   Now singeth, Sir, for Saintë Charity,
Let's see, can you your father counterfeit?"   *copy*

The fox's flattery works, and he acts quickly

This Chanticleer his wings began to beat,
As man that could his treason not espy,
So was he ravished with his flattery.
4515   Alas! you lords, many a false flatterer
Is in your court, and many a losenger,   *liar*
That pleasen you well morë, by my faith,
Than he that soothfastness unto you saith.   *truth*
Readeth Ecclesiast of flattery,   *a Book of Bible*
4520   Beware, you lordës, of their treachery.[1]
This Chanticleer stood high upon his toes
Stretching his neck, and held his eyen close,
And gan to crowen loudly, for the nonce,   *occasion*
And Daun Russel the fox starts up at once
4525   And by the gargat hentë Chanticleer,   *by throat caught*
And on his back toward the wood him bare,   *carried*
For yet ne was there no man that him sued.   *followed him*

Exclamatio!

O Destiny, that mayst not be eschewed!   *avoided*
Alas, that Chanticleer flew from the beams!
4530   Alas, his wife ne raughtë not of dreams!   *cared not*
And on a Friday fell all this mischance.
O Venus, that art goddess of pleasánce,
Since that thy servant was this Chanticleer,
And in thy service did all his powér,
4535   More for delight, than world to multiply,
Why wilt thou suffer him on thy day to die?[2]   *allow him*

---

[1] 4520 In this passage and in the one just below beginning O *Destiny* the Nun's Priest comes through strongly as preacher rather than as storyteller.

[2] 4536 O *Venus* ...: Friday is Venus's day, in Latin "Veneris dies," (in French: vendredi, Italian: venerdi). Venus is the goddess of sexual pleasure. Chanticleer, a devoted follower, makes love often and for sheer pleasure (*delight, pleasance*), not for offspring (*world to multiply*).

O Gaufrid, dearė master sovereign,[1]
That, when thy worthy king Richard was slain
With shot, complainedest his death so sore,
4540   Why n'ad I now thy sentence and thy lore   *knowledge & learning*
The Friday for to chiden, as did ye?   *to rebuke*
(For on a Friday soothly slain was he),
Then would I show you how that I could 'plain   *complain*
For Chanticleer's dread, and for his pain.

Epic comparisons with Troy, Rome and Carthage

4545   Certės such cry, nor lamentatïon
Was never of ladies made, when Ilion   *by ladies / Troy*
Was won, and Pyrrhus with his straightė sword   *w. sword drawn*
When he had hent king Priam by the beard,   *seized*
And slain him (as saith us Eneidos),   *"The Aeneid" says*
4550   As maden all the hennės in the close,
When they had seen of Chanticleer the sight.[2]
But sovereignly Dame Partelotė shright,   *loudest / shrieked*
Full louder than did Hasdrubalė's wife,
When that her husband haddė lost his life,
4555   And that the Romans hadden burnt Cartháge,
She was so full of torment and of rage,
That wilfully into the fire she start,
And burnt herselfė with a steadfast heart.
O woful hens! right so cryden ye,
4560   As when that Nero burnėd the city
Of Romė, cried the senatorės' wives
For that their husbands losten all their lives;
Withouten guilt this Nero has them slain.

---

[1] 4537 *O Gaufrid...:* "O Geoffrey, my dear and best master." The praise is, of course, ironic, like the rest of the passage. Gaufrid is Geoffrey de Vinsauf, author of a famous book of rhetoric in which he gave models for writings suitable for different occasions. In one of these he rebuked Friday for being the day on which King Richard the Lionheart was slain.

[2] 4551 *Certes such cry ...:* The women of Troy never made as much lamentation at the fall of their city as did the hens when Chanticleer was seized! Another set of mocking comparisons between the barnyard and several notable occasions in history: the fall of Troy, including the slaughter of King Priam and many others as told in Virgil's *Aeneid;* the destruction of Carthage, and the burning of Rome. Earlier the deceitful fox was compared to the great traitors of history.

Back to the barnyard. The widow and the neighbors give chase.

	Now will I turn unto my tale again.	
4565	The sely widow, and her daughters two,	*poor*
	Heard these hennès cry and maken woe,	
	And out at doorès starten they anon,	
	And saw the fox toward the grovè gone,	*go*
	And bore upon his back the cock away;	
4570	And crièd out: "Harrow" and "Welaway!	*(cries of alarm)*
	Aha! the fox!" — and after him they ran,	
	And eke with stavès many another man;	*sticks*
	Ran Coll our dog, and Talbot, and Garland,	*(dogs' names)*
	And Malkin, with a distaff in her hand.	*girl's name*
4575	Ran cow and calf; and eke the very hogs	
	So fearèd for the barking of the dogs,	
	And shouting of the men and women eke,	*also*
	They rannen so, them thought their heartès break.	*would break*
	They yellèden as fiendès do in hell.	*devils*
4580	The ducks cried as if men would them quell,	*kill*
	These geese for fearè flewen o'er the trees,	
	Out of the hivè came the swarm of bees.	
	So hideous was the noise, ah, ben'citee!	*bless us!*
	Certès he Jack Straw and his menie,[1]	*his mob*
4585	Ne madè never shoutès half so shrill,	
	When that they wouldè any Fleming kill,	
	As thilkè day was made upon the fox.	
	Of brass they broughten beams and of box,	*trumpets / of boxwood*
	Of horn and bone, in which they blew and pouped	*trumpeted*
4590	And therewithal they shriekèd and they whooped,	
	It seemèd as that heaven shouldè fall.	
	Now, goodè men, I pray you hearken all.	
	Lo, how Fortúnè turneth suddenly	
	The hope and pride eke of her enemy.	

---

[1] 4584 Jack Straw was a leader of the Peasant's Revolt (1381) in which a number of Flemings, craftsmen from Flanders, were murdered. This is one of Chaucer's very few political references.

The cock's quick thinking secures a reversal of Fortune

4595 This cock that lay upon the fox's back,
In all his dread, unto the fox he spak,
And saidė: "Sir, if that I were as ye,
Yet would I say, (as wise God helpė me):
'Turneth again, you proudė churlės all.   *wretches*
4600 A very pestilence upon you fall.
Now am I come unto the woodė's side,
Maugre your head, the cock shall here abide.   *In spite of you*
I will him eat, in faith, and that anon.'"
The fox answéred: "In faith, it shall be done."
4605 And as he spoke that word, all suddenly
The cock broke from his mouth delivery,   *deftly, quickly*
And high upon a tree he flew anon.

Undaunted, the fox tries flattery again

And when the foxė saw that he was gone:
"Alas!" quod he, "O Chanticleer, alas!
4610 I have to you," quod he, "y-done trespáss,
In as much as I made you afeared,   *afraid*
When I you hent and brought out of the yard.   *seized*
But, Sir, I did it of no wikke intent.   *wicked*
Come down, and I shall tell you what I meant.
4615 I shall say sooth to you, God help me so."   *truth*
"Nay then," quod he, "I shrew us bothė two.   *blame*
And first I shrew myself, both blood and bones,
If thou beguile me oftener than once.
Thou shalt no morė through thy flattery
4620 Do me to sing and winken with mine eye.   *Cause me*

The moral of the story, drawn by the protagonists

For he that winketh when that he should see,
All wilfully, God let him never thee."   *never prosper*
"Nay," quod the fox, "but God give him mischance
That is so indiscreet of governance,   *has so little control*
4625 That jangleth when that he should hold his peace."   *chatters*

The moral drawn by the narrator

Lo, such it is for to be reckėless
And negligent, and trust in flattery.
But you that holden this tale a folly,
As of a fox or of a cock and hen,
4630 Taketh the morality, good men.
For Saint Paul says that all that written is,   *Romans 15:4*
To our doctrine it is y-writ y-wis.[1]
Taketh the fruit, and let the chaff be still.   *grain / alone*
Now good God, if that it be thy will,
4635 As saith my Lord, so make us all good men,
And bring us thy highė bliss. Amen."

Here is ended the Nun's Priest's Tale

The Host is delighted at the tale but no more respectful than before.
He makes crude if approving jokes about the Priest's virility.

"Sir Nunnė's Priest," our Hostė said anon,
"Y-blessėd be thy breech and every stone;   *thy sexual equipment?*
This was a merry tale of Chanticleer.
4640 But by my truth, if thou were secular,   *a layman*
Thou wouldest be a treadė fowl aright.   *a real henrider*
For if thou have couráge as thou hast might,   *sexual prowess*
Thee were need of hennės, as I ween,   *You'ld need, I think*
Yea, more than seven timės seventeen.
4645 See which brawnė hath this gentle priest   *See what muscle*
So great a neck, and such a largė breast!
He looketh as a sparrowhawk with his eye.
Him needeth not his colour for to dye
With brasil, not with grain of Portingale.   *Red dyes*
4650 Now, Sir, fair fall you for your tale."   *bless you for*

---

[1] 4632 *To our* ...: "Everything that is written is written indeed for our instruction."

SELECT GLOSSARY / ENDPAPERS

AUTHORITY, Auctoritee, Authors: The literate in the Middle Ages were remarkably bookish in spite of or because of the scarcity of books. They had a great, perhaps inordinate, regard for "authority," that is, established "authors": philosophers of the ancient world, classical poets, the Bible, the Church Fathers, historians, theologians, etc. Citing an "authority" was then, as now, often a substitute for producing a good argument, and then, as now, always useful to bolster an argument. The opening line of the Wife of Bath's Prologue uses "authority" to mean something like "theory"— what you find in books — as opposed to "experience" — what you find in life.

CLERK: Strictly speaking a member of the clergy, either a priest or in the preliminary stages leading up to the priesthood, called "minor orders." Learning and even literacy were largely confined to such people, but anyone who who could read and write as well as someone who was genuinely learned could be called a clerk. A student, something in between, was also a clerk. The Wife of Bath marries for her fifth husband, a man who had been a clerk at Oxford, a student who had perhaps had ideas at one time of becoming a cleric.

CHURL, churlish: At the opposite end of the social scale and the scale of manners from "gentil" (See below). A "churl" (OE "ceorl") was a common man of low rank. Hence the manners to be expected from a person of such "low birth" were equally low and vulgar, "churlish." "Villain" and "villainy" are rough equivalents also used by Chaucer.

COMPLEXION: See Humor below

COURTESY, Courteous, Courtoisie, etc.: Courtesy was literally conduct appropriate to the court of the king or other worthy. This, no doubt, included our sense of "courtesy" but was wider in its application, referring to the manners of all well bred people. The Prioress's concern to "counterfeit cheer of court" presumably involves imitating all the mannerisms thought appropriate to courtiers. Sometimes it is used to mean something like right, i.e. moral, conduct.

DAUN, Don: Sir. A term of respect for nobles or for clerics like the monk. The Wife of Bath refers to the wise "king Daun Solomon," a phrase where it would be wise to leave the word untranslated. But Chaucer uses it also of Gervase, the blacksmith in the "Miller's Tale" and of the fox, Daun Russell, in the "Nun's Priest's Tale." And Spenser used it of Chaucer himself.

DAUNGER, Daungerous: These do not mean modern "danger" and "dangerous." "Daunger" (from OF "daungier") meant power — in romantic tales the power that a woman had over a man who was sexually attracted by her. She was his "Mistress" in the sense that she had power over him, often to refuse him the least sexual favor. Hence "daungerous" often indicated a woman who was "hard-to-get" or over-demanding or disdainful, haughty, aloof.

DREAMS: There was a good deal of interest in dream theory in the Middle Ages, and considerable difference of opinion: some held that dreams were generally inconsequential, others that dreams often were of considerable significance. Those of the "significant" school had biblical support from both testaments e.g. Pharaoh's dream of the fat cows and lean cows and Joseph's interpretation (Gen. 41) and many others in the OT, and in the NT , e.g. the other Joseph's dreams that assured him that Mary his wife was pregnant with Christ through divine intervention (Matt. 1:20, 2:13-20). They also had Macrobius's famous Commentary on the Dream of Scipio which distinguished between 5 different kinds of dream, 3 of them significant ("visio, somnium, and oraculum") and 2 insignificant ("insomnium" and " visum" or "phantasma"). The first 3 were felt to be prophetic in one way or another by Macrobius; the other 2 either simply carried on the worries or desires of the day, or were formed of disconnected and fragmentary images (phantasma) supposedly the result of indigestion. These last two, of least interest to the philosopher, might be of more interest to the psychologist and poet. Chaucer has several dream vision poems, in most of which he has some discussion of dream theory: *The Book of the Duchess*, *The House of Fame*, *The Legend of Good Women*, *The Parliament of Fowls*, especially the opening of *House of Fame* on the causes and significance of dreams. The argument of Chanticleer with Pertelote about the value of his dream in The Nun's Priest's Tale illustrates the common medieval disagreements, and brings up references to a number of the authorities that have been mentioned above. The most influential sources of the tradition of writing dream poems were Boethius's *Consolation of Philosophy* and the *Romance of the Rose*, a French poem of the early 13th century. Chaucer had translated both of these in whole or in part.

GENTLE, Gentil, Gentilesse, Gentleness: "Gentilesse" (Gentleness) is the quality of being "gentil" or "gentle" i.e. born into the upper class, and having "noble" qualities that were supposed to go with noble birth. It survives in the word "gentleman" especially in a phrase like "an officer & a gentleman" since officers traditionally were members of the ruling class. Chaucer seems to have had a healthy sceptical bourgeois view of the notion that "gentilesse" went always with "gentle" birth. See the lecture on the subject given by the "hag" in the Wife of Bath's Tale (1109-1176). But since "gentle" is used also to describe the Tabard Inn and the two greatest scoundrels on the pilgrimage, the Summoner and the Pardoner, one must suppose that it had a wide range of meanings, some of them perhaps ironic.

GOSSIP: (from Old English "God sib") literally a "God relation," i.e. a spiritual relation from baptism, a godchild or godparent. By Chaucer's time, it meant "confidant" with a flavor of our modern meaning to it.

HUMOR (Lat. humor—fluid, moisture)/ COMPLEXION: Classical, medieval and Renaissance physiologists saw the human body as composed of four fluids or humors: yellow bile, black bile, blood and phlegm. Perfect physical health and intellectual excellence were seen as resulting from the presence of these four humors in proper balance and combination. Medieval philosophers and physiologists, seeing man as a microcosm, corresponded each bodily humor to one of the four elements—fire, water , earth, air. As Antony says of Brutus in Julius Caesar "His life was gentle, and the elements So mixed in him that Nature might stand up And say to all the world 'This was a man'" (V,v,73-75). Pain or illness was attributed to an imbalance in these bodily fluids, and an overabundance of any single humor was thought to give a person a particular personality referred to as "humor" or "complexion." The correspondences went something like this:

Fire—Yellow or Red Bile (Choler)—choleric, i.e. prone to anger

Earth— Black Bile— melancholic i.e. prone to sadness

Water— Blood— sanguine—inclined to cheerfulness, optimism

Air — Phlegm — phlegmatic—prone to apathy, slow

Too much red bile or choler could make you have nightmares in which red things figured; with too much black bile you would dream about black monsters. (See Nun's Priest's Tale, ll. 4120-26). "Of his complexion he was sanguine" is said of the Franklin in the General Prologue. Similarly, "The Reeve was a slender choleric man" (G.P. 589). The Franklin's "complexion" (i.e. humor) makes him cheerful, and the Reeve's makes him cranky. A person's temperament was often visible in his face, hence our modern usage of "complexion." Even when the physiological theory of humors had long been abandoned, the word "humor" retained the meaning of "mood" or "personality." And we still speak of being in a good or bad humor.

LEMMAN: A lover, a sweetheart. Not a courtly term, but used by the likes of Nicholas and Absalom about Alison in the "Millers Tale," for example. The Manciple has a long gloss on this "knavish" word used of poorer women, but not to be used of ladies (unless they are trollops too). It is, he says, the equivalent of "wench." See Manciple's T. 205 ff.

LIKEROUS: Lecherous, though this sometimes seems a harsh rendering. In the "Miller's Tale" Alison has a "likerous" eye. "Lecherous" might fit there, though "flirtatious" is probably better. In the "Wife of Bath's Prologue" (732) it is used of Lucia who was so "likerous" of her husband that she killed him. "Jealous" seems a more accurate rendering here.

LORDINGS: Something like "Ladies and Gentlemen." The first citation in OED contrasts "lordings" with "underlings." "Lordings" is used by both the Host and the Pardoner to address the rest of the pilgrims, not one of whom is a lord, though the Host also calls them "lords."

NONES: For the Nones; For the Nonce: literally "for the once," "for the occasion", but this meaning often does not fit the context in Chaucer, where the expression is frequently untranslateable, and is used simply as a largely meaningless tag, sometimes just for the sake of the rime.

SHREW: "Shrew, shrewed, beshrew" occur constantly in the Tales and are particularly difficult to gloss. The reader is best off providing his own equivalent in phrases like "old dotard shrew' (291) or "I beshrew thy face."

SILLY, Sely: Originally in Old English "saelig" = "blessed." By ME it still sometimes seems to retain some of this sense. It also means something like "simple", including perhaps "simpleminded" as in the case of the Carpenter John in the "Millers Tale." The Host's reference to the "silly maid" after the "Physician's Tale" means something like "poor girl." and the "sely widow" of "Nuns Priests Tale" is a "poor widow" in the same sense. The Wife of Bath refers to the genital organ of the male as "his silly instrument."

SOLACE: Comfort, pleasure, often of a quite physical, indeed sexual, nature, though not exclusively so.

WIT: Rarely if ever means a clever verbal and intellectual sally, as with us. It comes from the OE verb "witan," to know, and hence as a noun it means "knowledge" or "wisdom" "understanding" "comprehension," "mind," "intelligence" etc.

GLOSSARY

(E): Refers the reader to Endpapers, a
Select Glossary (above), which has
fuller definitions of a few key terms.

A

A-back: backwards
A-bed: in bed
Amid: in the middle
A-night: in the night, at night
Anon: immediately
Array: clothing, finery
Apostle: Saint Paul or one of Christ's
immediate twelve followers.
Avaunt: boast
Aye: always, continually

B

Bear (wrong) in hand: deceive
Belle chose: beautiful thing (See **quaint**
2 and **quoniam.**)
Bencitee: Abbr. Lat: "Benedicite" =
"Bless (you)," "Bless (us)"
The number of syllables varies
with the line: ben-stee, ben-sit-ee,
ben-dis-i-tee, ben-e-dis-i-tee.
Bet: better
Blive: quickly
Boot(e): cure, benefit
Bren: burn
Buckler: shield
But (if): unless, only, except

C

Can: know how to, be able to
Cart: cart, chariot
Catel / chattel: goods
Certes: certainly
Cheap: v. to buy, n. market, supply
Churl: low born fellow (E)

Clepe, clepen, cleped: call, be called,
be named.
Coat Armor: the cloth tunic worn over
armor and often decorated with
the knight's coat of arms to iden-
tify him.
Could: knew (how to), was able to.
Past tense of "can."
Cuckold: a man whose wife is unfaithful; a figure of fun. Among other
things, he is said to wear horns on
his head.

D

Daungerous: cool, aloof (E)
Debt: in its conjugal sense, the obliga-
tion of one married partner to sat-
isfy the other's sexual need when
required.
Deem, deemen: think, judge
Defend: forbid, denounce
Degree: social rank, age
Doom: judgement, court

E

Eft: again
Eke: also
Ever each: each one, everyone
Eyen: eyes

F

Fabliau: short naughty story
Fain: glad
Fay: faith
Ferforthly: As far as, to the extent
Fetis: pretty, neat
Fine: finish, end
For-: this prefix is often "intensive."
"forwrapped": completely
wrapped up. "fordrunk": totally
drunk.
Forward: a bargain, agreement

G

Gan: began, but frequently indicates simply past tense
Gay: cheerful, fine, well dressed
Gentle, gentleness,: well-bred (E)
Gossip: literally a godparent or godchild, a confidant. (E)

H

Hent: seize, seized
Hest: command(ment)
Hight: called, named

I

Ilke; th'ilke: the same, the very
Inn: house

K

Kind: nature, birth
Kirk: church

L

Leve: dear, beloved
Lever: rather
Lest: = List
Lewd: ignorant, lay (as in "laymen")
Likerous: lecherous (E)
Like: please, "it liketh me" = "it pleases me"
List: wish, want; "Where God list": where God wishes. "List me not to write": I do not wish to write; "where him list": where he pleases.
Lordings: ladies and gentlemen (E)
Lorn: lost
Lust: see "list." Desire of any kind including sexual desire, pleasure. Also strong feelings, like grief (see Kn.T. 3063)

Luxury: (Lat. luxuria): lechery, sexual lust

M

Maugre(e): despite; "maugre his head (eyes)": in spite of his wishes
Methinks, methinketh: it seems to me

N

Nas, Nis = **N'as, N'is:** was not, is not
Ne: negative grammatical article
Nill or n'ill = ne will = will not
Niste or n'iste = ne wist = did not know. Past tense of "n'ot."
Nones, nonce: the occasion (E)
Not or n'ot = ne wot = does not know
Nould or n'ould = ne would = would not

P

Pardee: by God
Parson: parish priest, different from a friar or a monk

Q

Quaint (1) adj: odd, clever, devious, intricate
Quaint (2) noun: femal genitals; same meaning as next entry
Quoniam: female genitals (See **quaint 2** and **belle chose**)
Quit: repay, get even

R

Rede, redde: advice (noun), advise (verb)
Rown: whisper

S

Sely: happy, hapless, simpleminded, innocent (E)
Sentence: view, opinion, judgement, meaning
Shrew: wretch, nasty person (male or female)
Silly: See "sely" (E)
Sikerly: certainly
Sith: since
Somedeal: some part, somewhat
Sooth: truth, true
Starve: die (not necessarily of hunger)
Stint: stop
Suffer: allow, endure
Swink(en): to work
Swinker: worker
Swithe: quickly, very

T

Targe: shield
Thee (verb): to prosper, succeed;
   theech = thee ich = I prosper
   Also occurs as **theek** = thee ik
   so theek = so may I prosper
Think: to think, to seem
   Methinks = it seems to me,
   them thought = it seemed to them
Thilke: = the ilke = the same, the very
Tooth: taste, consumption;
   "**colt's tooth**": youthful taste
Troth: truth, word of honor
Trow: guess, think
Tway: two

U

Unethe(s) or **Unnethe(s):** barely, scarcely
Upright: face up

V

Very: true, real, absolute
Villain: man of lowest social order
Villainy: conduct thought to be typical of a "villain," ignoble or shameful behavior

W

Ween(en): think;
   past t. "wend" = thought;
   "they wenden" = they thought.
   Not to be confused with the next verb in this list.
Wenden: to wend (one's way),
   "they wend(en)" = they go.
Wher(e): whether, wherever
Whilom: once upon a time
Wight: creature, person
Wimple: a garment of soft cloth worn by women and which covered the neck and part of the chin and forehead. Part participle of the verb is "Y-wimpled."
Wisly: certainly
Wiste: knew: its negative is "n'iste" = did not know
Wit, Witen: knowledge, to know (E)
Wood: mad
Wot: knows, (negative: **n'ot**) = does not know

Y

Y-: a prefix generally indicating past participle
Ywis: certainly, indeed.